Looking
After Pigeon

Looking
After Pigeon

Maud Carol Markson

THE PERMANENT PRESS
Sag Harbor, NY 11963

For information, address:
    The Permanent Press
    4170 Noyac Road
    Sag Harbor, NY 11963
    www.thepermanentpress.com

Library of Congress Cataloging-in-Publication Data

    Markson, Maud Carol.
        Looking after Pigeon / Maud Carol Markson.
            p. cm.
        ISBN-13: 978-1-57962-187-2 (hardcover : alk. paper)
        ISBN-10: 1-57962-187-2 (hardcover : alk. paper)
            1. Fatherless families—Fiction. 2. Brothers and sisters—Fiction.
        3. Family—Fiction. 4. Domestic fiction. I. Title.

    PS3563.A6717L66 2009
    813'.54—dc22   2009014435

Printed in the United States of America.

For
Alec Thunder

Special Thanks

To my husband Burton who gives me the freedom to write, to my father, Aldan, who instilled in me a love of the written word, and to my friend, Harriet, who inspires me, and who gently and persistently pushed me in the right direction.

A Summer Story

Memory is an odd thing. When I was ten I broke my wrist in a bicycle accident and can remember none of the pain of the fall, the place where the bone came through the skin, or the inconvenience of having my arm in a white plaster cast for eight weeks. There is only a small scar. At sixteen I lost my virginity, and although I can trace the boy's face in my sleep—the slope of his nose, the definition of his chin, the curve above his lip—I have only a vague notion of his body. It could be any boy's body. In fact, there are entire blocks of time, years, that I have but little memory of at all. Perhaps a part in a school play comes back to me now and then, or the winter my brother and I learned to ski, but little of the day-to-day events, what people were saying to me, how I was feeling.

Except for the summer before my sixth birthday. For that summer I have almost photographic recall of the heat, the voices that surrounded me, the smells, all those incidents, particulars that took place. They changed me. To this day I am most restless during the summer months. While others are off on vacations, growing brown on the beach, playing tennis, swimming, I grow morose, often inert, thinking about the past.

"You should see a shrink," the man I live with advises me. "They're trained to help people like you get over things like that."

"I don't need help from some stranger," I tell him. I am resistant to professionals who believe they can see something in you that you cannot see for yourself. "We'll work this out alone."

But I can tell that he is tired of my moodiness. He wants to live a normal life. And so, he tells me, if I am not to go to the psychiatrist, I must at least consent to write my story of that summer down. He is practical that way. He is used to coming up with solutions for problems.

"You need to let that summer go," he tells me. "Exorcise it on paper."

I think I agree. At any rate, I love the man, I want to make him happy, and besides, he can be very persuasive. It is with all this in mind that I have at last taken his advice.

Sudden Departures

Our mother named her children after birds. Dove was the eldest, my brother Robin in the middle, and my name was Pigeon. I was last of all. Our mother lived in the city and knew little of birds, the beautiful names found in Peterson's or in Audubon's field guide to birds. She knew of doves, of course; they appeared in the Bible and on Christmas cards, and stood for peace. As a teenager she had worn a gold-plated dove on a necklace, and when her first child was born, easily, while she lay in a drug-induced state, she thought of the gold dove cooing near her ear. Five years later, following hours of hard labor, Robin came, and after still another five years I was the most difficult of all.

She gave my brother and me the names of city birds, the ones she had seen perched just outside her apartment window during each of her pregnancies.

"There is destiny in your names," she explained to us. "For all birds fly free. Even the pigeon."

"Only after he's landed a crap," Dove said.

"That is a very natural and free thing to do," mother assured me.

Robin smirked; Dove let out a heavy sigh.

Still, I believe, as I am sure our mother did, that the names we are given as children have much to do with the people we later become. Perhaps we do not really fly. It is done these days only safely aboard commercial airlines, and none of us have migrated far from home. Yet I am certain something of what our mother tried to impart in us at our birth is with us still, and always will be.

"You can change your clothes, and even have plastic surgery on your face," she would say. "But you cannot deny your own name."

Nor could she deny her past, although she often wished that she could. She had been only seventeen when she married our father. It was a story they repeated often. He had discovered her in a crafts shop in central New Jersey where she worked making and selling earrings.

"Your mother was so beautiful," father would tell us. "And so serious. She told me at first sight that fate had us both in its tight fists."

Our mother also told him that his cigarette smoking would lead to death and that the heart was a small and fragile organ in need of a wise and gentle touch.

She sold our father a pair of silver earrings and a matching ring, all of which he promptly gave to her in the same paper bag he had bought them in. Then he asked her out to dinner and waited all afternoon for her to get off work. He leaned against the wall of the small shop, puffing on one cigarette after another, and watched as she waited on customers, worked the register, and all too often brushed her red hair not away from her face, but across it, as if she had something to hide.

Later that night, on their first date, he realized she was the woman he wanted to marry, and he thought of ways to convince her to accept his offer. He told her she had hair like silk and a poignant face, eyes the color of wild grass. And he told her his parents were dead, that he had no relations to speak of.

"You must realize," mother told us. "He was not looking for someone to care for him, but someone to travel with him through the journey of life."

"I was a loner," father said, and that appealed to our mother's sense of independence.

She could not wait to leave her family home.

At a table covered with a thick white cloth, they ate steak and baked potatoes wrapped in foil and for dessert they had chocolate mousse. A waiter poured out red wine whenever their glasses were only half full. It was the most expensive restaurant in the area and our mother was duly impressed.

Towards the end of the meal, our father toasted their future together, and when our mother looked into his face she knew what was meant. He told her he was studying to be a pharmacist; that sounded respectable. And he assured her she would have a place to live. He rented a furnished apartment, and owned a black and white TV. He even promised to show her New York City. He had lived there his entire life and could give her a grand tour.

"I had never been there before," mother would tell us. "I imag- ined it held all the treasures in the world." And for a while it did.

Later, however, sometime after Dove was born, our mother realized she barely knew the man she had married and was hardly getting to know him any better. He worked long hours even then, and there was a baby at home, demanding and needy. Our mother didn't fit in with the young crowds in the West Village who were advocating free love and protesting the war, nor with the other mothers who walked up and down the streets, pushing their carriages and strollers ahead of them. And I believe she gave up trying.

She cultivated an eccentricity that denied her friends; there was no one she talked to over the telephone, or gathered with in the morning over a cup of coffee. The neighbors thought her odd. For she rarely went out, and she did not wear clothes like the other mothers we knew, but loud colors and scarves, tight black pants for someone much younger or dresses for someone much older. She spoke in pronouncements, rather than in ordinary sentences; she did not believe in celebrating holidays or birthdays.

"They are commercializations of our lives," she explained.

"So what, they're fun," Dove had said, and then, "I can't imagine you ever being seventeen. Ever being young."

"I had so many dreams," mother said.

And our father would finish for them both. "None of the dreams came true."

During my earliest years we all lived in a fourth floor apartment on the Upper West Side where our father worked as a pharmacist in a neighborhood drug store. I saw little of him during that time; he often had late shifts, and when he arrived home from work I was already bathed and in bed. I remember the soft hum of the televi- sion in the living room where Dove and Robin watched the evening comedies, and after they had welcomed our father, he would tiptoe in to wish me good night. Often I was already asleep and I would awaken to the crack of light as he opened my bedroom door. Then he would come near to me, sit by my side, and sometimes, if he were in the mood, he would sing me a lullaby. Usually they were American folk songs he had learned as a young child from his own father, who had played the mandolin, but there was one song—my favorite—that he had made up himself.

"I composed this the night you were born," father told me. "A hot September evening in New York." And then in his low scratchy voice, he would sing:

> There's a pigeon so white
> and another so gray
> I saw them just once
> before they flew away.
>
> They are strong as eagles
> and coo like doves
> and bring magical luck
> to those that they love.
>
> If at night I am quiet
> in hope they'll appear
> I may see their image
> in my sweet pigeon here.

I loved the pigeon song, its simple melody, its rhyme, and I knew the words by heart. Still, no matter how long I pleaded, he would never sing it to me on request. Only in the dark room when it was just the two of us alone.

"It's a night song," he told me.

"But the nights aren't long enough," I would always say.

Although often absent, our father was clearly the favorite among us children. He was twelve years older than our mother, and seemed older even than that, like a grandfather one rarely sees, but always misses. He spoke softly to us and listened when we told him of our days, of our lives. And he remembered what was said; he knew the names of Dove's many friends, asked her about them. He spoke to Robin about the science fiction stories he read, and advised me to enjoy my youth.

"It leaves so quickly," he said.

"We thank God for that," mother said in that brisk offhand tone she often used. "Don't you know it's unhealthy to be a child forever."

Our father had looked at her as if she were a sudden stranger in his house, sitting in his kitchen, minding his children, but surely no one he knew.

OUR MOTHER spent all her time in the apartment with us; she cooked and cleaned, watched what we put in our mouths, how often we went to the bathroom, what time we fell asleep. Yet she could not have told you where Dove went each day after school, or that even at ten Robin dreamed of becoming a doctor. And she knew little of how lonely I was in our small apartment; there were no other young children in the building and our mother was fearful of letting me out of the house alone. I grew well accustomed to playing by myself indoors; it has even served me well as an adult. I have never clung to men like some young women do, or to careers, or homes. Solitude is not an undesirable state, although alone all day with our mother as a child I often thought of it so.

It was our father who seemed to know what each of us might want or need. From the pharmacy he brought home cosmetics for Dove, and discarded medicine vials for Robin, who liked to pretend he was a scientist. For me, there was always candy and sometimes paper dolls or coloring books. It was I who emptied our father's pockets in the morning; he would leave his white pharmacist's jacket hanging over his chair in the kitchen and I would distribute the gifts while we ate our early breakfast.

"A new lipstick for Dove," I would announce and toss the silver tube her way. "Frosted peach."

Sticking my hand further into the pocket, I might pull out an emptied Benadryl glass. "This must be for Robin," and he would reach over to claim his prize.

"And the candy is for you," father said, pulling me into a hug, and I would cup the foil-wrapped chocolates in my fist.

"Not until after breakfast," mother frowned. She disapproved of these gifts; that is what she told us, that they spoiled not only our appetites but also our souls.

"Parents should be respected for their love and knowledge, not for the things they give," and she accented the word 'things' as if it left a nasty taste in her mouth.

"I respect Daddy," I said to her. I let the sweet chocolate sit on my tongue, melt down my throat. Dove rolled her eyes. She had told me her own version of the truth, that our mother was merely jealous, for there was never a gift in any of our father's pockets for her.

❧

As GENTLE and kind as our father was with us children, we soon learned he was also a crook. For years he had been dispensing illegal drugs to girls on diets, stressed-out businessmen, women troubled with nerves. Of course I did not know all this at the time; I was just five when the authorities discovered our father's crimes, took away his license, told him to move out of the area, preferably out of the state altogether. I only knew that our father was suddenly home in the middle of the day, and that something was terribly wrong.

For two months, February and March, our father and mother sat in the living room staring at each other, waiting for the money to run out. Dinner was never prepared and we subsisted on cheese and crackers or cold cereal and sometimes tuna fish. What little order the apartment had previously contained vanished; our beds went unmade, the laundry lay piled up for weeks, dust accumulated on the windows, under the couch, and all the ashtrays remained filled with our father's half-smoked cigarettes. We were old enough to take care of ourselves, of course, to clean the house, make simple dinners, but we did nothing. Once our mother and father stopped being parents, we also stopped, for a time at any rate, being their children.

Dove did not come home until late in the evening, slightly disheveled, not even bothering to tiptoe. Of course, I was used to my sister's boyfriends. Although still young, she had always been a beautiful girl. Like her namesake the dove, she was soft and fair, and she did not have freckles like Robin and me; her skin was always clear. She wore her red hair long and loose. And her shoulders, hip bones, even her cheeks were delicate and fragile as if they might crumble from the weight of her clothes or the careless touch of a hand. She inspired people, particularly men, to care for her—teachers at school took her under their wings, neighbors gave her gifts and inquired after her health, and of course there were always boys—as if she actually needed their help.

This time, there was a new boyfriend, she told me. And there was something in the tone of her voice, in the way she smiled, that made me believe there was something different about this one, something special.

"He's an older man," Dove confided in me one evening before bed.

"As old as Daddy?" I asked.

"Don't be ridiculous," she said. "But old enough."

She was getting ready for another date, and I watched as she combed her hair, slowly, all the way to the ends. Then, curiously, she swept her hair up with her hands, swung it around, and started combing all over again.

"Is that who you were with last night?" I said.

"Well, what do you think," said Dove. I thought that she was.

"What do Mother and Daddy think?" I asked. She had finally finished her hair and was now applying lipstick and then a spray of cologne at her neck and wrists.

"Who cares?" Dove said. And although she grinned at me, wide and friendly, I believed in some strange way she did care, that she was not quite as pleased as she appeared.

Our family's troubles had affected my brother as well. Robin, who was analytical and self-possessed, and who had always done well in his studies, was now being kept after school for truancy, and he brought home his first poor grade.

"What do you expect," he said to me, shrugging his shoulders. "How would you do?"

I did not know, only that I struggled with my own demons in the house alone; I started stealing change from our mother's purse and our father's pockets, although I had no use yet for money. I stopped eating at mealtimes, but sneaked the food into my napkin so that I might later eat it alone in my room. I sometimes went to sleep with my clothes on—cotton pants and shirt, my short white socks.

Still, our parents said nothing to us during these months, no matter how poorly we behaved, and little to each other as well. When they did speak, it was with anger and sadness.

"I can't believe you could be so stupid," mother sometimes said to our father. "I can't believe you got caught."

"I can't believe I did it at all," father said, but he did not deny his guilt. He told her he was lucky not to be imprisoned, and that if he had any strength at all he would have killed himself. "As they did once long ago to protect honour, family."

"What honour?" mother said. "If you kill yourself you're dead. That's all."

"I know," he said sadly, but he could not help himself from wishing he might.

We children tried to stay out of their way, but our apartment was small, and we were interested in our parent's dilemma, anxious to hear any news, for they did not share much of it with us. Despite our mother's frequent lectures and admonishments for living, neither of our parents actually believed in burdening their children with the personal facts of their own lives, and so in their silence we created a world far more frightening than anything they might have actually told us about. I'd rifle through my parents' drawers looking for clues, spy on them unawares from the doorway, run to the telephone first whenever it rang. On the few evenings when Dove was home, we would gather together in her bedroom. It was little more than a large closet, but the room's closeness, like a warm secret lair, inspired confidence and talk. We would sit, the three of us, on Dove's bed, and sometimes, although not very often, she would even take me on her lap, and all of us would share our many fears.

Dove was certain she would soon be taken out of school, and sent to work to support the family.

"I'll be a waitress in some dive," she said. She leaned back so that her hair fell over a rose-colored pillow with the words 'peace' embroidered on each side; our mother had made it the year Dove was born, and it had stayed in her crib and then on her bed ever since. "I'll never have fun again as long as I live," she said.

Robin worried that our father would be sent to prison surrounded by murderers, child molesters, large cruel men with scars on their faces and no teeth.

"I've read about the state penitentiaries," he told me. "Men aren't the same when they come out, if they come out."

"They don't send daddies to jail, do they?" I said.

"Shut up," Dove said to us both. "You don't know anything."

Perhaps we didn't, but what I imagined was very real: my entire world disappearing into our mother's Hoover vacuum, my brother, sister, each of my parents, one by one, being sucked up into that loud nozzle and then down through the hole. All but me. I was always left in the apartment alone, listening to the noise of the Hoover, the disappearance of my family and all our possessions, unable, and uncertain how to turn the power off.

I IMAGINED that my life, so fearful and strange, would go on like that for many years; our mother and father both home and out of work.

During the day, when Robin and Dove were at school, I was with my parents alone, and often, because they were so still, I went up to them, pressed my head against their chests, unsure if they were still breathing, still alive.

"An unoccupied child is a dull child," mother would sometimes say to me.

"Go play, Pigeon," father advised. "We need to be alone. There are problems to be sorted out."

I did not yet fully understand what it meant to pay rent and electric bills, or the grocery bills. But I knew the landlord had already threatened to evict us, that our telephone had been turned off for a while, and in the evenings the electricity flickered off and then back on.

"One day it won't come back on," Dove told me. "One day we'll all be left sitting in the dark."

But instead what happened was far worse.

I remember it was the third day of April, the first day of real spring smells and warmth, so that even in the early hours, as we slept, the sun shone through our curtains, making warm spots on our necks and faces. I was just waking up, or perhaps I had been up for hours. I often lay awake in bed, flat on my back, my arms folded across my chest, and I would stare up at the ceiling searching for animals or the familiar faces of people I knew in the shadows and light above my head. That morning while Robin breathed erratically in his struggle to awaken, I traced with my eyes the outline of a grey dog, the snout of a pig, and the long neck of a giraffe. Then, as if I had a premonition of what was to come, I saw the face of our father in the corner where the two walls met.

"Go back to sleep," he seemed to be saying. "Close your eyes." But it was too late. When I turned my head, Dove was already standing in the doorway. She was calling quietly for Robin and me to hurry, get out of bed, to wake up.

And when we did, she told us that our father was gone. In a voice utterly lacking in emotion, she said, "He's left us here alone. Completely alone."

"We still have mother," I said, and Dove rolled her eyes.

Robin was upright in bed now. His brown hair was curly from sleep and there was crust in the corner of both eyes. His face, long and serious, looked unnervingly like our father's, and scared. "Where did he go?" he asked twice. "Where did he go?"

"I don't know," Dove said.

She crossed the room and sat on the bed beside me. Ours was a small, unchanging room and I did not often notice it, but that morning I watched as my sister looked around—at the curtains that had hung there since the previous tenants, at the two twin beds with the maple headboards, at the walls, once white, but now graying and dull, covered with my crayon drawings—and the room seemed a sad place to spend so much of my life. My sister looked down at me, took me in her arms as if I were a young baby. She stroked my hair, and I felt her chest heave in an enormous sigh. She still smelled of the sample cologne our father had brought home from work not so long ago.

Robin slipped out of his own bed, came and sat next to her. Straight backed, clasping his pillow, he seemed unusually small in his cotton baseball pajamas.

"Mother showed me the note," Dove continued. "It said he's never coming back."

"You don't know," Robin said. He closed his eyes for a moment as if in thought. Then looking up, he said, "He's gone to jail."

"He did not go to jail," said Dove.

"Well, he's not going to tell you that he went," said Robin.

"He ran away," Dove said. She kissed me and her face was damp as if she had been crying. I didn't say a word; although I was unhappy about our father leaving, I was also, for the immediate moment, enjoying my sister's attention, pleased at her unexpected touch. I hoped she would not let me go.

"The note read that it was the best choice he could make," Dove told us. "The only choice. And that we are better off without him."

"We'll hear from him when he's on parole," Robin insisted.

"What's parole?" I could not help but ask.

"It means Dad will be out one day," Robin explained to me. "And he'll come back to be with us."

"Believe what you want," Dove said, tossing her head back in disgust.

"But you're not going to get any letters or phone calls. He's not going to visit us at Christmas. We'll never have our family back."

"Oh," I said, and Robin glared at her, his eyes squinting small.

And although we did not believe it at the time, Dove was correct. Our family was never the same again.

THERE WAS no memorial service for our father; he was not dead. There was no announcement of divorce. He was simply gone, and none of our neighbors or relatives came to express their regrets, there were no letters of condolence. In fact, his absence was rarely spoken about at all after that morning, although it was surely felt. Mother advised us not to mention or even think about our father again.

"Don't breed false hopes in your hearts," she told us. "Do not wish for what can never be."

Instead she told us she was looking towards the future; she was working on a plan to help our family out.

We were certainly in need of one. We had eaten eggs every night since our father had left, not omelets or even scrambled, but boiled so they sat on our plates like white Ping-Pong balls. Dove had slept at her new boyfriend's house twice; I saw her come in early in the morning just in time to change her clothes for school. The TV was failing and it stuttered with static. The landlord's visits were angry and frequent. Robin told me we were destitute, although I didn't know what the word meant at the time, and Dove threatened daily to move out altogether. Action surely needed to be taken, but we could not have agreed upon what.

Our mother made the announcement in our small living room. We were all told to congregate there while she stood before us in the center of the room, wearing the yellow silk dress she wore on special occasions, and her face was made up as if she were going out for the evening, blue shadow outlining her brows, bright red lipstick on her mouth. She had closed the drapes on the windows, lit only one lamp, so the room was dark and ominous, and she spoke in a voice barely higher than a whisper, as if we were about to be warned of some trauma or natural disaster waiting to occur.

Still, it appeared that only I understood the significance of the moment. Dove, leaning back on the couch, stretched her long legs out before her, stifled a deliberate yawn.

Robin giggled. "I know," he said. "We're all going with Dad to jail. To the family jail."

"That isn't funny," mother said, but she was undeterred. She cleared her throat, tapped her hand sharply against the coffee table for attention, and when she finally had it, she told us something that was to change each of our lives.

"We're going to move," she said. "Out of this apartment, out of the city, away from here."

"Move?" I said.

"Move where?" said Dove.

"We're going to live with your Uncle Edward at the beach," mother said.

"Who is Uncle Edward?" Robin asked. "Did I ever meet him?"

"You met him when you were a young boy," she continued. "He owns a large house in New Jersey, and since he has no family of his own, he has kindly welcomed us into his home."

"The beach!" I said. I had been to the seashore only once that I could remember. But that day—with both my parents and that sudden unexpected brightness of the sun and the sand and the vast ocean—was as vivid and as real as any of the days I had spent since.

I remembered our father carrying me on his back into the cold water, first to my feet, then my legs, and finally up to my waist and chest, so that I held my breath at the sudden sting of water and salt. Later, we all helped build a large sand castle, complete with tunnels and moats, and I had watched fearfully as the waves drew up closer and closer, praying silently that they would never reach us, though of course they did.

"Someday I will live in a castle like that," Dove had said towards the end of the day, and she had stared wistfully at the wet mounds in the sand. All that was left of our afternoon's work.

Later, our mother gathered up our belongings, and Dove and Robin took one last swim in the ocean. I sat beside our father on the sand; he had pointed out the boats sailing on the horizon, promising to one day take me on a ship—a voyage across the seas. And tucked between Dove and Robin on half a seat, I had fallen asleep on the long train ride back to the city, dreaming I was on a boat, one with colored sails that rocked back and forth and back and forth.

Now, at mother's news of the move to Uncle Edward's, I jumped right up on the couch.

"I would love to go to the beach," I said. "It would be a dream come true."

"Who asked you?" Dove said.

"Sit down, Pigeon," mother said, and the barrage of questions began.

"What about our apartment here?" said Robin. "What about all our stuff?"

"It's not as if we owned it," mother said.

"But what about school?" said Dove.

"It's almost summer," mother said. "And in the fall you will go to a new school. A school near your Uncle Edward's house."

"Will Daddy come too?" I asked. I still kept expecting him to appear.

"Your Daddy is gone," mother said.

"To jail," Robin said.

"To a better place," Dove said. "Than here."

"There's no better place than the beach," I said, but no one else agreed.

THAT NIGHT, we packed. In retrospect I do not know why we were in such a hurry—I suppose my mother had not paid the rent or electric bill—but at the time I thought that was how everyone moved. In the middle of the night, packing feverishly, taking only what was necessary. Leaving most everything behind.

"You can each fill one suitcase and no more," mother told us.

"I thought Uncle Edward had a mansion," Robin said.

"Don't talk back," mother said.

"I need more than one suitcase," Dove said. "I can't possibly leave everything I own behind."

"Possessions are a necessary evil," mother said. "The fewer the better."

Dove shook her head, and looked as if she were going to cry.

"You can have room in my suitcase," I told her.

"Oh, shut up," she said, but I knew she was not angry with me. That was just the way she spoke when she was upset or hurt, or confused. And when I made my offer a second time, she smiled and placed two books of poetry by e.e. cummings and a new sweater on top of my one case. The sweater was pink and soft and expensive looking and as I placed it among my own small belongings, I wondered where it had come from, how Dove had acquired such a beautiful thing.

After we were finished packing, our mother called a taxi, and when it arrived, we loaded our luggage and a few assorted boxes into the trunk.

"I cannot believe we are taking a cab," Dove said. "To move."

"Would you rather take a bus," mother said, but I do not think she expected a reply.

So that is how we traveled to our new home, by a dirty Checker Cab, out of the city, over the bridge, and south to New Jersey. We were all quiet on the dark ride. Our knees touched, our feet were buried beneath boxes, and we could barely move our arms. None of us asked when we would reach Uncle Edward's, it was not that kind of expectation; but we all counted the minutes in our head, and each of us wondered what our new life would be like.

Though situated on the beach, Uncle Edward's was not a mansion, or even a very large house. It was little more than a bungalow, built twenty years earlier, and looking twenty years older than that due to the ravages of the salt air, the winter storms, and years of subtle neglect.

"Is this where we're going to live?" Robin asked.

The four of us were standing on the sidewalk in front of the house. It was a dark night and the quiet street was deserted.

"Where's the ocean?" I said, for though we could smell the salt air, hear the roar of the waves, we could see nothing in the distance.

"I want to go home," Dove said. She was not alone; perhaps we all thought of turning back, going home, even our mother, but the cab driver had already pulled away from the curb, headed north towards the bridge, back to the city where we used to live.

"It will look better in the morning," mother assured us all.

"I doubt it," Dove said.

"It will look better inside," mother said. And instructing us to each carry something, anything, into the house, she led the way up the path and through the front door.

There were four bedrooms in Uncle Edward's house, a small dark kitchen, and a living room with sliders that opened out towards the ocean. On the living room floor (as well as, I discovered, throughout the entire house), instead of carpeting or wood, there was linoleum.

"It's easier to keep clean," mother explained to me. "Particularly in a beach house."

"But not nearly so nice," I said.

The house was sparsely decorated, with odd pieces of furniture placed at angles and in assorted corners. There were blinds in the windows, but no curtains, and the lights were all too bright. It appeared as if Uncle Edward had arrived there one day, dropped off his few belongings, and then left again. There were no pictures on the walls, no photographs or books. The best thing that could be said about the house was that it was clean, immaculately scrubbed, and still smelling of ammonia and Lysol.

"Remember, Edward is a bachelor," mother said. "And a salesman. He is rarely home."

"I can see why," Dove said, and she looked around the living room, rolled her eyes, shook her head.

"This isn't much bigger than our apartment," Robin pointed out to us. "If you measure in square feet."

Then Robin paced the rooms as if he *were* measuring it, with his feet, and his footsteps, but he said nothing.

"And we're in the middle of nowhere," Dove added.

"We are?" I said. The sudden thought of being stranded, without my bed, my familiar room, without the apartment that had been the only home I had ever known, so thoroughly exhausted me, I fell to the cool floor in a small heap.

Our mother took my arms in both her hands and pulled me to my feet. "Stand up, Pigeon," she said to me. "We're at the beach. The ocean."

"The ocean in the middle of nowhere," Dove said.

"Let's not talk of that now," mother said. "The important thing is that we're home."

But it did not feel like home to any of us, and would not for quite a while.

Uncle Edward

In my life, I have always been taught what must be kept and saved.

"Not much," mother instructed us. She is dismayed by the materialism she sees around her—people scurrying to possess more and more as if that were their sole purpose in life. Always buying, buying. Cramming their high-priced purchases into barren homes.

"I had such high hopes for my own generation," mother would sometimes go on. "But now we are the worst offenders."

Only our mother has held on to her ideals. Even before our father left and we had no money, she bought only the essentials. Enough clothes to do wash just once a week, but no more. One toy perhaps at Christmas and another on my birthday. Books could be borrowed from the library, she told us. There was certainly no reason to actually keep them. She did not even buy food in quantity, although that might have been more economical. Instead, she went grocery shopping often, and bought small amounts—enough for two dinners, lunch, a breakfast as if she had to worry about spoilage, or more likely did not expect to live in one place very long. Some might claim she was merely stingy or tight, but looking back, I do not believe this was so. Instead, I believe our mother truly wanted to be free of all encumbrances, like a saint or a monk, or like Gandhi, as if that would make her pure or happy, or save her for some spiritual afterlife.

"Possessions ground you forever," we were told. "Keep you embedded in commercialism and waste."

"You say that as if it's a bad thing," Dove replied.

Even the gifts we received from others, family members or friends, were often thrown in the trash or given away to the needy. We quickly learned that any item left out in our mother's view—Robin's new pen, Dove's bottle of cologne, my four glass Arabian horses—were disposed of, simply gone one day, as if they held no more value or significance than a used-up carton of milk or a sweater pilling and grown too small.

"That was cluttering up the house," mother would always answer when asked where our new belonging had gone. "And what did you really need it for anyway?"

I must admit I did not understand why it was wrong to want new toys, clothes, more of anything in fact. Dove told me our mother was crazy, that if we weren't meant to buy new things, there wouldn't be any stores. To me that made sense. But what I did learn from our mother was the value of secrecy, of keeping what was most important well hidden, stored safely away. To this day, there is much I don't tell even those I am closest to—my views on God, my ridiculous optimism for the future, the way I really feel when I am touched. And whenever I buy something new, be it a dress, a book, or even a box of cookies, I will at times hide it from myself for a few days, even for an entire month, until it is no longer fresh, no longer subject to disappearance. This may sound odd, I know, but I am always amazed anew to discover that what I hid is not gone, not thrown away, but simply waiting for me where I left it.

Back then, though, like many children, I was more systematic. I had a box of treasures I kept under my bed, and though the box's contents sometimes changed—I would add something new or decide to remove an item I had tired of—I always knew exactly what was there at any one time, knew even their importance in my life.

That was why, when it was time to leave for Uncle Edward's, I was not at a loss, like Dove and Robin, as to what to pack. I already knew what had to be brought with me, and even how much room each item would take up in my allotted suitcase. I did not question that these were the things that could not be left behind.

I woke up that first morning at Uncle Edward's in a strange bed in a strange room, but to the familiar high-pitched voice of our mother.

"Pigeon," she was shouting, so that I woke immediately upright in bed. "What have you done?"

I could not imagine what I had done, unless of course I had walked in my sleep, shouted something rude during the night, or perhaps overslept. I worried often that I did do these things. Or maybe it was already the middle of the day and everyone was waiting, impatient and angry, for me to wake up.

"Get out of bed," she said. "And look at this. Right now."

It was then that I saw what our mother was shouting about. She was kneeling on the floor by the bed, stooped over my suitcase, its precious few contents spilled out beside her knees. I saw Dove's new sweater first, and then I saw my own belongings—a stuffed dog with a bright red nose, a copy of *A Child's Garden of Verses*, a map of the New York subway system, a discarded jewelers box containing the ticket stubs from the two movies I had gone to, five matchbooks, a validated train ticket, and cards from my last birthday given to me by Dove, a sympathetic neighbor, and my father. There was a coloring book and a box of barely used crayons, a pad of paper with a picture of an elephant I had drawn and was proud of, my toothbrush, my favorite blue shirt, and the last tin of candies my father had given me before he left. Only five of the chocolates remained.

"What is all this junk?" mother said, without so much as allowing me to answer. "Where are your clothes? Where is your underwear, socks? What have you packed?"

"You said to only pack what was essential," I said, but I could already see it was no use. I had done something terribly wrong.

She was not yet dressed, still in her robe and bare feet, but she had already showered. I could see how her light hair was darkened where it was wet and she smelled strongly of soap. Stooped over on the floor, she studied my belongings, her jaw tense, her shoulders like small sharp wings at her back. She picked up the train tickets and the movie stub and felt them between her fingers as if they were so much ash.

"I cannot believe you could be so stupid," she finally said. "I don't know what you expect to wear."

"I don't know either," I said sadly. Although none of this had seemed important the night before when I packed, and still did not bother me nearly enough now.

"Well, you should," she said. She was looking at the birthday cards now, looking at the pictures on the front first—a rabbit, a girl holding a balloon, then reading who they were from on the inside. When she got to the one from my father she crumpled it in her fist.

"Don't do that," I said, leaping from the bed. For a moment my nightgown, like a damp towel, twisted around my legs, but then I was free. Tearing the birthday card from our mother's hand, I held it close to my chest.

"It's mine," I said. That was the first time I had ever spoken back to her, and I experienced a sense of power I imagined others must feel when they ordered me about. My heart beat quicker. I felt suddenly brave. "Don't you touch my things," I continued in a voice that came from somewhere else. "They're mine."

"No, this is yours," mother said, and without any other warning, she rose up and hit me across the upper part of my arm. She used the flat palm of her hand so that it made a loud smacking noise, and as if that were not enough, she did it again. Our mother had never hit me before, never hit any of us children as far as I knew. And even though it was not very hard, for a moment I could see her hand print even after she lifted it away.

Later, during those first months at Uncle Edward's, I would remember that mark on my arm and think of it with a perverse kind of pleasure, whenever I was most angry at her, most hateful. As if her one act of violence justified any malicious thoughts I might ever have. But that morning, the stinging burn of her hand only made me choke and then pull back at the pain, and when I finally caught my breath, I cried and cried.

"I'm sorry," I said. "I'm really really sorry."

"You should be," mother said in a dry voice. "You really really should be."

Then she cupped her hands around my neck, her long fingers pressing at the nape and under my chin as if she were going to choke me, or even pull me into an embrace, although she did neither. I was still crying, but we stared at each other, like boxers before a match, or like two angry dogs, as if the fight was not finished, but just begun. We stood there for only a few seconds, though it seemed longer, and her look (one I had seen her give often to Dove) was one I also came to know well; it was resentment for what I had made her become: a mother.

It was during this moment with her that I first met my Uncle Edward. Out of nowhere, he strode into the room with Dove and Robin behind him like soldiers following their leader into battle, reasoning a victory on the element of surprise. He did not look at mother, but only at me, and with one swoop he lifted me up into his large arms.

"Stop crying," he ordered, but in a deep gentle voice, and he smelled the way I imagined woods and earth and grass smelled. "Nothing can't be fixed or cured."

I didn't stop crying all at once, but I did feel better. I burrowed my head deeper into my uncle's chest and took one long peek at our mother. She was still on the floor, her robe billowing out around her knees like a tent. She was very carefully returning each one of my scattered possessions to my suitcase, as if by doing so she could reverse what had just occurred between us, and like a movie on a projector wind even further into the past, back to where I could no longer remember.

She stopped repacking when she reached Dove's sweater, held its softness in her arms as if it were an animal or a child, only to finally toss it carelessly onto the bed. With that she closed my suitcase up with a click.

All the while Uncle Edward continued to reassure me. "Don't cry little Pigeon," he said, until I wasn't crying. "Nothing is going to hurt you now."

"No one has hurt her," mother said in a voice unlike her own—deferential, frightened. She looked up at her brother not with anger, but resignation. "I know what you're thinking," she said. "But we were all fine before, and we will all be fine again."

"I certainly expect that," Uncle Edward said, and in words I will always remember, he made a short prayer, "I hope to God you will all learn the healing power of the sea."

"I like that," Dove said.

"Healing," Robin repeated.

Our mother shook her head, and although she rose up at last from the floor, it was only to sink down again exhausted on my unmade bed.

"Edward," she said, and then she repeated it as if it were a strange word on her tongue. "Edward."

"Yes, Uncle Edward," Dove beamed. "This is our uncle."

And Robin said to me, "Aren't you surprised? We thought he'd be older."

"We thought he'd be uglier," Dove said.

"Our family doesn't believe in ugly," Uncle Edward said.

"They thought you'd be different," mother said.

"I imagine I am," he said.

From the way they spoke, I suppose Dove and Robin must have considered it strange being there with our uncle who, in all our years, we had heard so little about. But it was not as if there were other relatives in our lives. I knew our father's parents had died when he was young, leaving him first with an elderly aunt and then when she too died, in a state home for boys. We thought it must have been terrible for him, but he had assured us it was not.

"There are far worse things than not having a family," he told us.

"Like what?" Robin had asked, "Like starvation, like being given the Chinese water torture?" But our father shrugged and did not answer.

We knew even less about our mother's family, although we understood they were still alive.

"Yes, I have parents," she had told us when prodded.

"We didn't think you were immaculately conceived," Dove said. "We know you *have* parents."

"And I have a brother as well," mother continued.

"But where are they?" Robin had asked. He always wanted to know the facts; he always had more questions than Dove or I, more questions than anyone cared to answer.

That day, he looked at our mother squarely, head on. "Why don't you ever see your family?" he asked her.

"Don't you miss them?" I said.

"They live in New Jersey," mother said, as if that explained most everything. "And I don't want to see them. I don't miss them at all."

We were all younger then, had experienced less, and we looked at her as if she had just said she would be giving each of us away. It was frightening hearing our mother say she didn't miss her own family; for all our arguments and yearnings we couldn't have possibly imagined not missing our own.

"Families can be a terrible burden," father had answered for her. "They can make you into someone you're not."

"We had a falling out," mother said simply.

And I had imagined our mother on top of a high hill; she was waving to her family, her mother and father, her brother, and they in turn waved back to her.

"Good-bye, Joan," they called. They were each of them falling down the hill, rolling far and away into a grassy abyss. "Good-bye. Farewell," they all shouted, as they rolled over and over, their bodies picking up speed in their descent. Falling, falling out.

Maybe that wasn't what had happened at all. It could have, though, for we had never heard from our mother's family on holidays or on our birthdays. There were no phone calls or letters, and only sometimes a clue, a small hint that they existed at all: a gold cross in our mother's underwear drawer, a mention of an illness, a brother passing again through the city (should they meet?), a faded photograph of a pretty red-headed girl and boy holding hands in front of a small white house. Now Uncle Edward had not only appeared in our lives, but we would be living with him here in his home. And the surprise was not that he existed, but that it seemed as if he had always been there just waiting for us to arrive.

I would have liked to stay in Uncle Edward's arms longer, but when he finally put me down, it was gently like a skater placing his partner smoothly and precisely on a sheet of ice. It was then that I looked up at him fully for the first time and I realized he was the most handsome man I had ever seen. He was perfect. He was dressed that morning in a silk smoking jacket and black velvet slippers. He was very tall, even in our tall family, and his hair was a much deeper red than our mother's, his nose narrow, his lips full. His eyes were so green I imagined the ocean, itself, had turned them that color, and I dared to hope, in time, if I lived here at the beach long enough, my own brown eyes might change as well. I knew he was only a few years younger than our mother was, but he looked much younger than that, and when he smiled I felt suddenly warm inside. I had never before looked at a man the way I looked at Uncle Edward—not as an uncle—but as a beautiful stranger standing before us leading me into a better life.

That morning, however, after we had all dressed, he led us only to breakfast. To a nearby diner owned by a friend. At a large corner booth in the nearly empty restaurant, we ordered stacks of pancakes, bacon, sausage, and home fried potatoes.

"I'm starving," Robin said as we waited for our food.

"Not starving," mother corrected. "You're hungry."

"Don't you ever feed these children?" Uncle Edward asked.

When the pancakes arrived, I poured big puddles of maple syrup across my entire plate, stuffed forkful after forkful into my mouth, not stopping to talk or barely breathe, and Uncle Edward even allowed me my first taste of coffee.

"She'll be wired as a puppy," mother said, but he paid her no mind. Instead, he encouraged us all to eat more, to order dessert if we so pleased.

Although he asked us about ourselves, what we liked to do, he did not wait for our replies, but talked about himself instead.

And even Dove, who prides herself on listening to no one, sat there silently waiting on each of his words.

We learned he was involved in sales, although we never learned exactly what it was he sold. He informed us there were important people in his life, people who paid to not have their identity revealed; they relied on him and trusted his silence. He traveled, although we were never told where. His work had taken him all over the country, he told us, and sadly had prevented him from ever settling down, raising a family.

"Perhaps you're not missing as much as you think," mother said.

"Shhh," Dove admonished.

"Your mother never believed in establishing roots," said Uncle Edward.

He told us he did, and that he had finally bought this house two years ago and, when he was able, lived at the beach not because it was convenient, but because he loved the ocean.

"It is one thing to visit the beach for a day during the summer," Uncle Edward explained. "And still another to spend your vacations by the sea. But it is entirely different living at the beach all year round. It is a quiet life, shops are closed for the winter, and the streets and beaches are deserted. The air is sharp, the wind strong, and the damp sting of the salt water is felt even indoors."

I thought he spoke like a poet, as if all the lines our mother had given us over the years had been refined in her brother's speech, made musical and new again.

"Of course I am not here nearly enough," he went on. "My work is always taking me from what I love."

"But what exactly do you do?" asked Robin, who perhaps was not quite as dazzled with Uncle Edward as Dove and I.

"He already told us," Dove said.

"I'm not sure he did," said Robin.

"I wouldn't want to bore you with all the details," Uncle Edward said, and he threw back his red-haired head and laughed.

Robin rolled his eyes at me, but I ignored him.

And mother, who had barely spoken during the entire breakfast, finally said, "You were always one for secrets, Edward, weren't you?"

"Weren't we all," said Uncle Edward.

At one point during our meal, his friend, the owner, came over to our booth to meet us. He was a large man, broad shouldered, with white white teeth, and fleshy lips, and when he saw our mother, he winked.

"So you're Ed's sister," he said.

He mussed my hair when we were introduced, and cuffed Robin on the back of his neck.

"Hey, big guy," he said to Robin, although Robin was short for his age that summer. "You sure are a handsome big boy."

When he arrived at Dove's seat he lingered even longer. With his massive hand he felt my sister's chin and cheek, and I saw his fingers brush her lips. I waited for Dove to tell him to stop, to snap back with one of her sharp replies, but she said nothing, as if she noticed his touch less than the buzz of a fly. Or worse, as if she liked it.

The man told us his name was Joe Winter. Winter, like the season. And let it be known, he continued, that any relatives of Edward's were welcome any time day or night to eat in his diner.

"As long as we're open and as long as you pay," he said to us, and roared at his own humor.

I disliked the man immediately, and assured myself he and Uncle Edward were not close friends. But before Joe left our table, he placed his hand on the nape of Uncle Edward's neck, whispered something in his ear, and they laughed together for what seemed like a long time.

After breakfast we followed Uncle Edward across two wide avenues empty of cars, and out onto the boardwalk, where I got my first good look at the ocean.

"This is my lifeline," he told us, and he brought me up to his shoulders, where I had never felt so tall.

It was still early in the season, and except for a few long-legged birds, the beach was deserted and the ocean was dark grey and angry as it spit its foam over the sand, leaving cut shells, seaweed, and pieces of trash all along the shore. I could smell that peculiar salt air and even taste it on my lips, and though it was sunny outside my face felt suddenly damp. When the waves crashed particularly loud, I put my hands over my ears.

"It scares me," I said.

"Everything scares you," Robin said. He had shimmied up onto the railing that separated the boardwalk from the beach, and he hung his legs precariously over the side. Robin was scared of little, Dove nothing at all.

"You will learn to love the sea," Uncle Edward promised me.

"Yes, they are easily adaptable at her age," mother agreed.

"Like sand poured from a bottle into a bowl," said Uncle Edward.

"Youth," mother said, and Uncle Edward repeated it after her, as if it were a code word between them for something they did not want us to hear.

Then, he and mother finally looked at each other, and they smiled as if they were suddenly remembering the same thing, an event in their own youth. It was the first time, since I had met Uncle Edward that morning, that I really could believe that he and our mother were brother and sister, that they had actually shared a childhood, common memories. They even looked for a moment alike—the red hair, the same long chin, their eyebrows sand-colored and arched.

We stood there, the five of us, for quite a while, looking out towards the sea. At one point, a sailboat passed by on the horizon; Uncle Edward pointed it out to us, and told us it was a pleasure boat going south to Virginia or perhaps even Florida.

"That must be the life," Dove said.

"Boats are one of the slowest modes of transportation," Robin said.

But Dove ignored him. "It's how I want to travel someday," she said.

We spoke of other things too. Mother mentioned the price of the cab ride the night before, and worried about where to buy groceries, and how to pay for them. Uncle Edward pulled out a shiny billfold and handed her ten twenty-dollar bills. We all watched, we all counted.

Robin asked how many people lived in the town, where would he go to school, was there a nearby hospital, and if Uncle Edward had a television set in his room. He told us he did and that it was a color one. At one point Dove even looked at Uncle Edward and said perhaps it would not be as bad as she thought.

"I don't believe it will be," Uncle Edward said. Then we walked the boardwalk back and forth, as if we were just any family out on a Sunday stroll. I, atop Uncle Edward's shoulders looking out towards the sea, Robin, as always, a few paces ahead, and Dove a few paces behind, our mother, head down, her hands shoved in the pocket of her old red coat, too warm for the late spring weather, never quite keeping pace with any of us.

I was not yet ready to go back to the empty house when Uncle Edward finally directed us home. I liked being on his shoulders, liked the scuffing sound the footsteps made on the wood, liked listening to the hum of conversation below me. But he told us he had to leave in another hour or so and not only that, but that he would be gone for a few weeks.

"Where are you going?" Robin asked.

"But we just met you," Dove said.

"You're leaving now?" I said.

"Children," said mother, her voice shrill again. "Stop shouting."

"Business calls," Uncle Edward said. "It always interferes with pleasure."

"I thought business was your pleasure," mother said mysteriously.

"Ah, if it were," Uncle Edward said.

We would eventually grow accustomed to his sudden appearances—hear his car pull up in the dark of the night, or look up startled during dinner to see him come in unexpectedly, and sit down before us waiting for a plate of food of his own. Of course, his disappearances would also become a matter of course. They might occur after only a two-day stay at home, and then sometimes he would be with us for more than a week; but when he left it was always quickly—perhaps during a game of cards, an aborted walk on the beach, before the bedtime story was completely through.

"Business calls," he would always say as he jumped up from whatever we were doing to pack. "Work awaits." Then he would be gone.

I adjusted to his leaving as I did to any difficult change, thinking first I would never survive and then going to bed one night realizing I had forgotten to think of him all day. But that first morning when he left us was the hardest. After we arrived back at the house, he packed quickly, throwing a few things into the trunk of his car, which I could see was already filled with luggage, shirts still in boxes from the laundry, a suit on a hanger, three boxes of shoes. Then we all assembled out in front of the house, and he waved, saluted even, and kissed each one of us good-bye. When he came to me, I clung to him, as if I had known him all my life, screaming for him not to leave.

"Don't go, Uncle Edward," I said, swinging my arms around his neck. "Please don't go." I had never felt I would miss anyone so much, more than I had missed our father even, and more than what really made sense considering we had only just met.

"I'll be back," he said to me, and then kneeling down so that his eyes met mine, he whispered in my ear. "I promise you, my special Pigeon. I'll be back."

Our mother finally had to pull me off Uncle Edward's leg and hold me down as he got inside his car, pulled out, rounded the corner, and drove away.

"I cannot believe you are acting like such a baby," mother said to me. "You barely know Uncle Edward. How can you possibly miss him?"

"But I don't want him to go," I continued wailing. "I want him back."

"You're such a crybaby," Dove said. "Grow up."

It was true; I was a bit of a crybaby. But I had less control over my tears than I did over hunger or thirst or the need to use the toilet. It was a bodily function. Just like when the doctor hit my knee with his hammer, and my leg jerked up in response, crying was a reflex that occurred whether I willed it to or not.

I DO not know that we quickly adapted to our new lives at the beach, but I do know that each of us settled into a routine. Perhaps it was not how we would have liked to spend our time; it seemed particularly rough on Dove, who spent a good part of each evening writing letters to someone back in the city. I would watch her lying on her bed in the room we shared, a pad of paper in front of her, a pen poised between her fingers as she painstakingly composed each line. Sometimes she sighed for greater effect, and when I asked her what was wrong, she told me that only in time would I understand.

"My heart is still in the city, " she said to me, and I imagined her heart really out of her body, filled red with blood, shaped like a valentine, and pulsing within the windows of our old apartment.

Our mother had decided not to enroll Dove and Robin in a new school for the last few weeks, and so their days were their own. At first I was glad, for I thought they would spend more time with me, but soon I realized it made no difference at all.

Dove had applied for a waitressing job at Joe Winter's diner, but it did not start until the summer, and in the meantime she waited inside the house for the summer crowd to arrive, activity to begin. Dove was not a girl who liked solitary pleasures—reading, cooking, needlepoint—but was most herself in front of other people, as if she were a television set, filled with entertainment and even glamour, that was made to wait blank and empty until someone came to turn her on. Dressed in her robe and sometimes her pretty pink sweater, she would sit at the window or on her bed, arms crossed over her chest as if she were cold, doing absolutely nothing. I do not know how she sat so still for so long. She always seemed sad.

Robin had his own activities, and after he left the house early in the morning we usually did not see him again all day until dinner. He would arrive out of breath, his cheeks glowing, strangely quiet, as if all his questions had finally been answered.

"Where do you go?" I once asked him, and "Won't you take me with you?"

"I guess someday I will," said Robin, but he did not tell me when.

Even mother got herself a job. She worked now at the local movie theater, every matinee and most evenings as well. She sat outside in the booth selling tickets, and then while the picture ran she went inside to work the concession stand. When she came home late at night, her feet made a squelching noise as they stuck to the linoleum, and her breath and hands smelled of popcorn.

"This job isn't forever," she told us. "It's just until I find something better. Something more suited to my talents."

"And what kind of talents are those?" Dove said.

"How much does the job pay?" Robin asked.

"Let me worry about that," mother said. "All my concern."

I was not sure I believed her, but I certainly tried not to worry. For I had more freedom than I had ever had before; I was left to go anywhere, outside to the beach, into the quiet town, down the long stretch of boardwalk. I saw the boarded-up stands that in the summer would sell salt-water taffy, corn dogs, ice cream, fudge, each of their signs proclaiming 'City's Favorite,' 'World Class,' 'Best on the Boardwalk.' I did not yet know what salt-water taffy was nor a corn dog; I imagined that they tasted good and planned out a strategy for the summer, how I would sample each and every one. It bothered me for a moment that I had no money of my own, but at age five money problems seemed easily overcome.

On sunny afternoons I went behind Uncle Edward's house, where the boardwalk did not go, and out onto the beach. At first I was still easily frightened by the crashing roar of the waves, but I soon grew used to it, and even began to like the constant sound of water hitting the shore. I would take off my sneakers and wiggle my toes like sea crabs, and then make footprints where the sand was still cool and damp. I dodged trash that I did not yet have names for—empty bottles of Jim Crow, discarded tampax, a used-up condom—and I collected shells and pretty stones, and colored glass made smooth by the salt and sand. I would wash the glass off in the water and, holding it up to the sun, peer through it at birds or the row of houses along the beach, and sometimes out to the sea when a boat passed by; and the colors of the glass would reflect and bounce so that the object no longer appeared familiar and mundane, but as something beautiful from another world.

I was used to being alone, and so did not feel particularly lonely. But I did feel much older than I had in the city. I was tall for my age, and most days wore an old pair of Robin's jeans cuffed at my ankles. Walking by myself during the day, I imagined that people seeing me thought I must be nearly nine or ten already, and then I imagined that I was orphaned, that not only had my father left, but my mother as well, and even Dove and Robin were gone.

"So brave," the people in the streets would whisper about me. "All alone in the world and taking care of herself."

They had no idea I lived in the small yellow house at the end of the block, and that lunch would be waiting for me on the table when I returned home about noon.

We had lived at Uncle Edward's house for two weeks to the date when the postcard arrived. It was addressed to all of us children, each of our names squeezed in the small space allotted. And it was from San Francisco. On the front of the card there was a photograph of a cable car filled with people, and as the cable car descended it looked as if it were not moving on the ground, but floating backward over the hill and then down towards the bay below. The card was from our father.

By chance we were all home when the mail arrived that day, sitting at the kitchen table, grumbling of boredom, and eating from a large tub of popcorn our mother had brought home from the theater the night before. It was the jumbo size and cost two dollars. She was back at work now until the evening, and we were together in the house, alone. The windows were open wide and a breeze was blowing across our faces. I had dropped a few stray kernels on the floor and on the front of my shirt, and Dove had already told me to pick them up or she would clean the floor with my face.

"Nice talk," Robin said.

It was he who went and got the mail, and he who held the post-card first close in his hands and then out for us all to see.

I looked at the picture, studying the people on the cable car as if one of them might possibly be our father, then down at the words San Francisco spelled out in bold white print along the top of the card.

"Is that where Daddy lives now?" I asked.

"Let me read it," Robin said.

"No, I'll read it," Dove said. "My name is first."

Robin thought for a moment before surrendering the card to Dove. But when it was safely in her own hands, she took her time, tracing her finger slowly over each of the letters in San Francisco, then turning it over to study the stamp, the postmark and date, pro-longing the inevitable. Finally, she dramatically cleared her throat and began.

"Dear Children," Dove read. And under her breath, "As if I'm really a child."

"Go on," Robin said. "Stop stalling."

"Dear Children," Dove read again. "I hope you are all enjoying the beach.

Watch out for rough water. And I will somehow see you soon." Then she stopped.

Is that all?" Robin said. "Is that all he wrote?"

"It's not a very big card," I said.

"He could have said more than that," Dove said.

"But what does it mean?" Robin asked. He was shifting his weight from one foot to the other. At one point he looked as if he might even topple over. "Is Dad coming back? How will he see us soon?"

"How should I know?" Dove said.

But Robin would not give up. "Do you think he'll live here with us?" he went on. "Or will we go to San Francisco?"

"Where is San Francisco?" I said.

"Ask someone who cares," Dove said.

Even Robin stopped for a moment to look at her, to consider our sister's pretty face, cool and impenetrable. "I wonder what he means by somehow?" he finally said.

I think we all wondered.

Then we sat back down at the kitchen table. I cupped a fistful of popcorn into my mouth, deliberately chewed it noisily, and thought about our father. I tried to imagine him in San Francisco, but I did not know what he looked like there. I saw him, instead, in our old apartment. He was sitting next to me on my bed, my small hand in his large one. His chin scratched my face when he got too close and he was singing my song. Suddenly, though, I could not remember the words, and for no other reason, I started to cry.

"Shut up," Dove shouted at me. "I am so sick of you crying all the time."

"Okay," I said, and for once I really did stop crying immediately.

Dove offered Robin and me one more good look at the card. I saw our father's neat handwriting, large and clear so that even I could read his words. I saw where he wrote 'Love Dad' and under it, in parentheses, his name—Alan. Finally Dove took the card back again, and in a voice threatening, yet also calm, she told us we were not to tell anyone about the postcard, not Uncle Edward, not anyone we met, and particularly not our mother.

"Not a word to her," Dove said, and she slipped our father's card into the top of her shirt where it was suddenly hidden from view, gone. As if it had never arrived at all.

"Why not?" I said.

"Don't be stupid," Robin said.

I felt sick from eating so much popcorn, suddenly could not even stand its buttery odor. I wiped my mouth with the back of my hand, felt the air from the open window and took a deep breath. I did not care about telling our mother, but I would have liked to tell Uncle Edward when he returned. Asked him to explain the postcard, what our father meant; I knew he would understand.

"Don't even think about telling anyone," Dove said to me as if she read my mind, and taking my face in her hands, she said, "Don't blow it, Pigeon. Just don't blow it."

"I'm not going to blow it," I said, twisting free. They were both staring at me now, their faces warning, and also challenging me not to make a mistake.

"I'm good at keeping secrets," I said.

We all were. Our mother never heard about our father's first postcard or the ones that eventually followed. Although it might have occurred to us that it must have been she who had given father our new address, that *she* must know where he had gone. But for the longest time, we felt that only Dove and Robin and I knew our father still existed. Knew he was not dead or in prison, but only waiting somehow for passage to return.

New Friends

Uncle Edward's town was strictly for tourist trade and summer residency. It was too far from the casinos in Atlantic City to attract their patrons, and not scenic or isolated enough to be a winter haven for nature lovers or loners. It was merely a summer tourist town, and as the days grew longer and hotter, we began to see signs that the season was clearly approaching.

All along the boardwalk and in the town proper, shop owners had returned to squeegee their windows, scrub floors, restock their shelves. Signs were placed in all the doors saying HELP WANTED and APPLY HERE. Realty offices reopened and were busy showing rental units to families who returned each year and to groups of college students who would lease by the week. Even the beach got a thorough cleaning. Two old men carrying plastic bags stalked the shore each afternoon picking up trash from the sand with the speared end of their long poles. People in uniforms came down to test the water for pollutants, and I watched them with their black cases, test tubes, and grim faces as they entered their findings in a spiral-bound notebook, day after day.

Dove began waitressing. Joe Winter's diner would not begin its summer hours for another month, but he told Dove she needed time to train, and that she could also be useful in helping him prepare his place for the tourists' arrival. Print up new signs and menus, inventory supplies, squeeze in an additional table, another three stools at the counter. Like all the other girls, she would begin with the breakfast shift and gradually, as she gained experience, work her way up to lunch and then dinner, when drinks were served and the tips were larger. Joe Winter did not think it would take a girl like Dove very long.

"Believe me, honey," he told her. "It's not because of Edward that you got this job. It's because you're qualified."

Of course, he also informed her, the qualifications for waitressing were few indeed.

This did not bother Dove. She started the first Monday in May, and when she returned home that afternoon, she was flushed, and even trembling.

"I made twelve dollars just in tips," she said to me as she kicked each of her shoes off, and then nudged them with her toes until they were out of sight under her bed. I had followed her arrival home, from the front door, up the stairs, and into the room we shared, and I listened to her attentively now, though I was not nearly so thrilled with her new job as she was.

"Joe told me this was just the beginning," Dove said, and she pulled a wad of bills out of her pocket and held them out for me to see.

"Joe?" I said. "You call him Joe?" It was not like it is today. Back then we did not call any adults by their first name.

"That's what he told me to call him," she said.

Her face was shiny, with a thin layer of perspiration; she wore a yellow and white uniform, an apron with large scooped pockets, and white opaque stockings. Her hair was pulled back in a net. On Dove, even this style was attractive.

"He said I'm too old and he's too young for any Mister."

Hearing this, I imagined she had mopped the floor with a little more gusto, cleaned invisible crumbs off the counter, made a fresh pot of coffee though the existing one was still half filled. Her slim hands moved quickly, darting here and there. She had nodded at all that Joe said.

"Believe me," he had told her, swinging a large friendly arm around her waist. "You're a part of the family now."

"He told me I was part of the family," Dove repeated, her voice breathy and low.

"What family?" I said. I was confused enough about my own to be able to clearly fathom why anyone would want to be a part of someone else's.

"Don't you know anything?" Dove said. I could feel her eyes examining me, much as I often examined my own face in front of the mirror. She would see my dark brown hair cut blunt at my chin, the dark eyes, see that my nose, my cheeks and chin were not delicate like her own, but sharp and prominent. Even from a distance you could tell I was too tall for my age and wearing boy's clothes that would never properly fit. No one would ever guess that Dove and I were sisters.

"The youngest one is attractive," I had heard people concede in whispers. "Even pretty in a strange way, but nothing like the older one. She's the looker." What did that mean—in a strange way? It was certainly not anything anyone whispered about Dove.

Curving her fingers over her palms, she studied her own pale nails. Then with one tug she took off her hair net so that all her fine hair fell loose and free, and the net sprang up into a small web that she put into her apron pocket. She lay back across her bed, not as if she were tired, but merely because she enjoyed the stretch. She squeezed her arms around her thin shoulders and held herself tight.

"He told me I was his friend," Dove said to me with a pleased, self-satisfied smile.

"Really," I said.

"He said I would fit right in."

I knew what our mother would say to this, if she had heard Dove.

"There is no advantage in being like everyone else," she would have said to Dove, to all of us, in fact. "Like lemmings jumping into the sea. You should treasure your eccentricity."

That is what our mother would have said; she had said it many times before, always including Dove among our family's strange members as if Dove were at all like the rest of us. But Dove would never be strange, eccentric. She was not one about whom people would be caught remarking: 'She marched to the beat of a different drummer.' No, Dove may have been beautiful and she may have been a particularly rebellious teenager, but despite her name, she was never a rare bird.

I listened to her chatter on—more about Joe Winter and waitressing—and thought only how much I would have liked to keep her home with me, not allow her to go back to work at the diner. I climbed onto the bed next to her, admired her uniform, its pure crispness, its authority, and worried about her and her new job. Worried about Joe Winter and the way I had seen him touch my sister's chin, her lips, as if they were *his* to touch, and the way he had cupped his big hand around the nape of Uncle Edward's neck, and his laugh, which was not a friendly laugh to me. I certainly knew I did not like Joe Winter, would never like him.

"He scares me," I said to Dove.

"Everything scares you, Pigeon," she said, pulling me over, muscling me down, so that I was lying next to her on the bed. She scooped my head in her hands and pulled me close so that our eyes met and I thought she might kiss me on the lips, although she didn't. I could feel the heels of her hands pressing against my temples. Her eyes were a most beautiful blue. Her pale face looked as fragile as the bones in a small creature's back—just one quick snap and the animal is dead.

"I don't like him," I said to her.

"Hush, Pigeon," she said.

But I repeated it. "I don't like him."

"You know," she said. "Sometimes you worry me."

Her voice was not angry, but dismissive, so that I was all the more startled, when without warning, she swiftly pushed me off the bed. Considering the act, it was not performed aggressively, but with deftness, as if she were merely a dancer completing her series of positions. I did, however, land with a bump, flat on my rear, my feet flailing out in front of me.

"Hey," I said, as if it were a hiccup.

Then I really did hiccup, just twice, and loudly, and I sat there where I had fallen, puzzled as to whether I was more hurt by the fall or by the fact that Dove had pushed me.

That deed done, she curled into a fetal position and closed her eyes.

"You don't even know what scares you," she said without looking up. "But I know what scares me." Then she did not speak again, and I had no choice but to stand up, straighten my clothes, and leave her in our room alone.

Dove was right, of course. At the age of five I did not know why I was scared of so many things. I knew only that I still believed that people who were different from me, from my family, were to be feared; and everyone was different from us—the children who had gathered to play outside our old apartment in New York, the mothers sitting out on their stoops, their laughter high, their whisperings, and their husbands who came home to join them in the early evening, tugging at their ties, rolling up their sleeves.

"Don't go near those people," mother had always warned me. "Their kind of values are contagious."

I was not sure what my mother meant, but those families did scare me, in the way they huddled outside their homes like a gang of teenage boys, plotting revenge, protecting their turf.

"You don't want to become like them," mother had always said.

I had no way of knowing yet, of course, that soon I would want to be like them. But Dove and Robin were older, had made friends and lost them. They knew the importance of friendship, of fitting in.

"Why can't you be like the mothers of my friends?" Dove often said to her. "Why can't you behave like them? Why can't you be like them?"

"We are originals," mother went on.

"We're freaks," Dove said. "A sideshow attraction."

I believed my sister was exaggerating. I hoped she was. But I really had no way of knowing. Was I so very different from the other children? Up to then I had had no method of comparison. Were my family freaks? We were the only family I knew.

The next night our mother worked late at the movie theater, and Robin, Dove, and I ate cold ravioli out of a can for dinner.

"I saw seagulls eating a crab right out of the shell," I told them as we sat in the small kitchen.

It was where we always congregated now, around the pale Formica table that filled up the room with its six straight-backed chairs, as if we were always expecting guests, or more food to be served. Other children, I later learned, gathered in the afternoon and evening in front of the television in a den or living room. But although we liked TV, particularly the sitcoms about families, the one set in the house was in Uncle Edward's room and we felt strange going in there by ourselves, like trespassers, intruders. There were no chairs in his room or carpeting on the floor, and so when we did go in occasionally to watch TV, we were forced to sit on his bed with its dark sheets and masculine spread. Although the bed was always made, the sheets clean, I sometimes thought I could smell Uncle Edward, or what I remembered to be his smell.

"I know what I smell," Dove would always say.

"She means sex," Robin said.

"Can you just imagine all that has gone on here," Dove said. Robin and I were no longer watching television but looking at her, trying to imagine for ourselves what she might see. Robin and I knew little of sex in those days, only what Dove had whispered to us from time to time in that superior way of hers.

"Like what?" Robin would sometimes ask. "What has gone on?"

"Like you'll ever know," Dove said.

Robin would blush and I would try to put all the things I knew about men and women and marriage and babies into one thought until I was thoroughly confused, and so distraught I would leave the room before our half-hour program was finished. It was awkward for all of us at best.

It was in the kitchen, that neutral and monochromatic place, that we felt most comfortable, most free to be ourselves. Tonight, I had managed to mash all my ravioli into an orange and brown stew in my bowl. I thought some more about the seagulls.

"They flew up in the air and dropped the crab so that it smashed open," I told Robin and Dove. "They pecked at it with their bills."

"Don't make me sick," Dove said. "We're eating."

"What we're eating makes me sick," Robin said.

He stabbed an orange ravioli with his fork and flicked it over onto my plate so that sauce spilled onto the table, splattering my shirt.

"Hey," I said.

"You're such children," Dove said.

"You think so," Robin dared her. "You think I'm a child." Then, listen to this, he seemed to say. As if he had been just waiting for an opportunity that evening, some point where he could tell us what it was he had been planning to tell us all along. He paused that extra moment for our attention—for me to finish chewing, for Dove to stop fingering the gold chain around her neck—before he spoke about his new friend, a woman he had met last week on the boardwalk.

This was not the first time Robin had mentioned her to us. He had teased us by making comments about her—told us she was older, but not by how much, told us she was brilliant, but not where she had gone to school or where she worked. He promised us we would meet her one day, but he had not yet told us when. "When she's ready," he always said. He would not even tell us her name.

Tonight he revealed to us a strange new piece of information: he told us she was a fortune-teller. "She can see the future," he said.

"A fortune-teller?" Dove said. "Oh, really." She began clearing our dishes, scraping what was left of our dinner into the trash, piling the plates one on top of the other into the sink. She was pretending not to listen to Robin anymore, but of course she was.

"Her name is Edith," he said. "And she tells fortunes on the boardwalk.

She reads palms and tarot cards and even owns a crystal ball."

"You believe that crap?" Dove said. With a sponge she wiped the table; her hand made large circular motions across the smooth Formica. "There are no such things as real fortune-tellers. They are all con artists," she said.

"You want to bet?" Robin said.

"I want to meet her," I said.

I had heard about fortune-tellers in the books that our father used to read to me—those all-knowing seers who reveal to the poor beautiful girl that she is really a princess and indeed she is. They warn the young boy not to go into the cave or the castle and when he disobeys as they predict he will, he is met with tragic consequences. I certainly believed in fortune-tellers.

"You can meet her tomorrow," said Robin. "Tomorrow when Dove gets off work."

"Will you really bring us to see her?" I said.

"He said he would," Dove said.

"Edith said it was time," Robin said.

"Oh, really," Dove said again, but I knew she would go.

WE ASSEMBLED the next day where the boardwalk began; five steps led up from a patch in the street, up to the slatted wood and the metal railing, and if you looked far up the boardwalk you could see how it lay straight, the ocean on the side, the various shops and stands on the other. I was there first waiting, and then Dove, still in her uniform, and she kicked at the railing so that it resonated in the warm wind.

"I can't believe I'm doing this," she said. "A fortune-teller."

But when Robin arrived, running down the boardwalk, out of breath, to meet us, she made no comment. We followed him to finally meet his friend.

Edith lived, and also worked, out of a small dilapidated storefront a mile north up the boardwalk. She had one of those doors I had only seen in picture books, the kind that you can open up from the top or the bottom, or if you so choose, all in one, both top and bottom together. She did not invite us in right away, but stared at us from the top half, as if determining whether we were really friend or foe, or worthy of her time, or as I later decided, as if she was determining our future.

I had always imagined fortune-tellers in high turbans and colored silks with big gold rings in their ears. But Edith was dressed in nothing like that. Instead she looked like a middle-aged woman who had few resources for nice clothing or jewelry. She wore an old button-down cardigan that was unraveling on one sleeve and a simple blue skirt. Her hair was long and graying and it hung in one braid down her back. She could have been someone's mother, wife, or aunt. More likely she was a woman without family looking for just one more way to make a living. The sign outside her door read:

FORTUNES TOLD, FUTURE READ
$20/EACH
OTHER SERVICES AVAILABLE

Robin bounced on the balls of his feet, his body like a quivering and excited dog. "I've brought them," he said.

"I can see you have," Edith said. Her voice was gruff as if she had smoked too many cigarettes, and she peered at each of us.

"Come in," she finally said, and we waited while she unlocked the rest of her door and opened it, taking us each by her cool hand into her home.

It was dark inside and it took awhile for my eyes to adjust from the brightness out on the boardwalk. It was just one small room; in the corner there was a sofa bed and in the opposite corner a hot plate and refrigerator. In the center of the room sat a round table covered with a lavender cloth. I imagined this was where she gave the fortunes, though there was no indication that there was anything special or magical about this table. In fact, there was little in the room that might have spoken of who she was or what she did.

The only strangeness at all that I could detect lay on the walls. They were covered, all four of them from floor to ceiling, with photographs of people, color and black and white, glossy, clear and fading yellow with age. Some looked like studio portraits, others only snapshots taken by a proud father of his children, or a husband of his wife. There were weddings, and graduations, Christmases, and birthdays, first dates, first born, new cars and new homes. Hundreds upon hundreds of people I had never met nor seen, looking at me, at all who entered, from their fixed place on the walls. These people in the photographs were no relation to me, and from the quantity and disparity of their faces, probably no relation to Edith either. And yet, this did not matter, for I was suddenly privy to the most meaningful moments in each of their lives.

Dove and Robin were looking at the walls too, although I imagined Robin had seen them many times before. But it was difficult to look away; each face, each person was compelling; all had something to say.

"I see you like my photographs," Edith said.

"Where did you get them?" I asked.

"Did you steal them?" Dove said.

"Some of them were given to her," Robin answered. "But most were thrown away, retrieved out of the trash, or fires, or left abandoned in homes for sale or stores going out of business."

"Yes, people are callous, and so careless with their lives," Edith said.

"Robin tells us you tell fortunes," Dove said. She had her hands on her hips.

"I don't tell fortunes. I see the future. I was cursed with the gift," Edith said, and she and Robin smiled knowingly at each other.

"Are you going to tell us our fortunes?" I asked.

"Are you going to charge us?" Dove said.

Robin shrugged, and Edith took him close to her, spread her fingers to his cheeks. Then picking up his hands in her own, she turned them palm upward and held them out for Dove and me to see.

"Your brother has fine lines," she said. "So fine they can barely be seen. He is the invisible child."

"I wish he were sometimes," Dove said.

"Go get the chairs," Edith said to Robin. "It's time."

As if by magic Robin produced four assorted chairs and placed them around the lavender table. It was as if he had already done it many many times.

We each took a seat, and Edith stared at us until even Dove was shifting uncomfortably. I looked at the photographs and for a moment had a terrifying thought that they were all pictures of people whose fortunes she had once told and in doing so had later possessed—not only the photos but the people themselves. Were they under the floorboards? In the closets? Behind the walls?

"Let me see your hands," she said to Dove, and as she had done with Robin she took my sister's hands and placed them palm to the ceiling. Edith's own hands were unusually large for a woman of her size, worn and callused. They looked particularly unattractive next to Dove's.

"Don't you have to do something first?" Dove said. "Don't you have to use a magic wand or say some enchanted spell?"

"Edith doesn't need artificial apparatus," Robin said. "She's the real thing."

"No hocus pocus," Edith said.

"So tell me," Dove said. "What do you see?" We were all, the four of us, now looking into the lines in her hands, seeing their length, their curve. We waited.

"You are a smooth receptacle," Edith finally said. "One that is transformed by what it holds—too much desire, and later too much pain."

"That's not me at all," Dove said, and she took her hands back, hid them inside the crook of each elbow. "I'm not so malleable."

"Is that what she said?" I asked.

Robin shushed me with his finger and Edith stroked her chin as if in thought.

Dove rolled her eyes.

"I told you she was a fake," Dove said. "I don't know why I even bothered to come."

But none of us left: we remained seated at the table. I curled the cloth up and down in my fingers. It was my turn next.

Edith's hands were surprisingly warm now as she touched me, bending her face over my small palms, looking for something no one had seen before. For the longest time she said nothing but traced the lines in my hand with her index finger, so rough that I was not sure she wasn't creating new lines there, ones that had never yet been. And even after she looked up she still remained quiet.

"Maybe Pigeon's too young," Robin said.

"No," Edith said.

"Maybe she sees an incredibly short life line," Dove said. "One that ends this afternoon."

"Stop it," I said.

"I see something," Edith said, sounding almost like an exasperated mother, like our mother sounded when she'd finally had enough. She looked at me. I shivered, and then she told us what she saw.

"I see a cunning, secretive child," Edith said. "One who believes she can rearrange the lives of others. Take control, play God. That is truly evil."

I felt my wrists go weak from the weight of her reading. My hands slipped onto the table with a silent thud. Robin smiled, a large forced smile. Dove did not. I could see the blue vein at her temple, the flush at her cheeks.

"No, you are the one who is evil," Dove said to Edith. "Pigeon is only five."

Then she rose from her chair so quickly that it fell to the floor with a clatter. Taking my arm, she jerked me out of my own seat. "We're leaving," Dove said. "We don't have to listen to this."

Robin bit his lip and held his breath for more than a few seconds. I believed if he were less sure of himself he would have had great misgivings about bringing us here to meet his friend. But he stayed fast, did not move, said nothing.

Years later he confided in me that Edith had been merely teasing me that afternoon in her shop; she had seen nothing in the lines of my young hands. No one believed I was really evil. But it was too late; the seriousness with which she had made her accusations remained with me. I truly believed there was evil in what I often tried to do—alter people, make their lives different—and I certainly believed it that afternoon.

As Dove and I left that day, Edith shouted to us. "Robin should have warned you," she said. "Knowing the future does nothing to prepare . . ."

Her last words were lost to us as Dove and I reentered the world outside. Oddly enough it looked no different; the sun was shining just as brightly. The waves still crashed down onto the sand. The old men were still out there on the beach stabbing at loose pieces of paper, their green garbage bags flapping in the breeze.

"Don't just stand there," Dove said. "Follow me." And I did, taking two steps to her every one, keeping my eye on the white of her uniform, the heels of her shoes, following her all the way home.

Once there she left me, went into our room, shut the door. When she eventually came out she was no longer wearing her uniform but jeans and a tee shirt, and she was carrying a letter with a New York address.

"Stop moping around," she said to me.

I was moping, sitting on the stairs, wondering how long it would be until dinner. I would count to one hundred, beating each number on the wall of the stairwell with my fist, and then I would begin over again. I did that often as a child, and later still as an adult—counted as a way to force the passage of time, in doctors' offices, for a phone call, for the results of an exam or review. As if counting was part of the penance of waiting, making me finally more worthy of deliverance.

She listened to me for a moment—"forty-eight, forty-nine," before shouting.

"Forget everything," she ordered, and then she was out of the house, perhaps only to mail her letter, but gone.

As if the afternoon had not been eventful enough, that evening our mother walked home from her job at the movie theater with a strange man. I was already in bed by the time they arrived at the front door, but I could hear them talking through the open window. Her voice was high, the gentlemen's low, and at one point they both laughed at the same time. I could not hear what they were saying, but I knew it was certainly a great deal more than good night. I lay there listening for a while as the wind, instead of taking their voices away, seemed to bring them closer and closer to me.

Who was the man she was with? I knew it was not Uncle Edward, and perhaps it was only her boss, whom I had been introduced to one afternoon, or maybe it was even Joe Winter. Then, in a hold-your-breath kind of thought, I wondered if it was our father.

The room I shared with Dove was in the front of the house and when I got out of bed and went to the window I saw them. They were standing close together, their backs to the house, as if shielding their identity. I could tell immediately it was not our father. This man was shorter than our mother, although I suppose not really short, but small shouldered with a narrow waist. He wore a white dress shirt, dark trousers. Our mother was in a bright orange dress. Earlier Dove had told her it made her look like a pumpkin, but she did not look like a pumpkin to me now. She was animated, her hands fluttered at the hair at the back of her neck, she slipped her foot in and out of her shoe. The man tossed his keys up into the sky and caught them, then he jingled them in his pocket as if they were change. There were a few times I thought he might leave (I think he said good-bye twice), but he kept coming back as if he had forgotten something, swiveling on his heels, extending his arms. I even saw his face—dark eyes and a moustache, and a round unformed chin.

I thought of getting Dove or Robin to show them this strange man—they were in Uncle Edward's room watching TV—but I dared not leave. I suspected something might happen, and then just when I thought he was gone for good, he came back again and kissed her. Kissed our mother right on the lips, as if he were our father, she his wife.

Thankfully, he did leave then, after the kiss, walking down the street throwing those noisy keys up in the air and down, and with a pop of his wrist up in the air again.

I did not breathe until he was out of sight. I heard the front door open and close and mother's voice saying, "I'm home." I saw the front outside light flick off, and sensed one in the kitchen being turned on, and then I heard her go into the downstairs bathroom, the toilet flushing, and then the rush of water as she turned the shower on. Robin and Dove continued to watch TV.

I might have gone back to bed, to sleep, might even have lain awake another hour until Dove came in and joined me in the room. In the dark, we might have talked about what I had seen outside. Dove would have laughed.

"He must have been ugly as sin," she would have said. "Anyone who kissed our mother."

"He had a moustache," I would have said. "He wore a white shirt."

But I did not wait for Dove. The words of the fortune-teller were still too fresh: "You are a cunning, secretive child," she had said.

I did feel cunning and secretive after what I had seen, after what I had thought. So, I did not wait, but instead tiptoed barefoot down the stairs, and then with a quiet turn of the knob, I slipped like a cat at night through the back door of Uncle Edward's house. Dressed only in my nightgown I walked out past the street and onto the beach and crept to where the dry sand met the wet, where the tide, for now, stopped. And there I sat.

I had never been to the beach at night, and certainly not alone. I could hear the ocean far better than I could see it, but if I looked north up the beach I could see the many lights from the hotels and apartments and various houses that dotted the shoreline. In the other direction, all was dark and quiet. There were only a few lights there, from private homes, and most of those were switching off now as the hour grew later. I could feel the wind sweep up my nightgown, but I was not cold. And although I was scared, of the ocean, the dark, of all that I did not know, I did not cry.

Instead, I prayed. I prayed for Dove and Robin to be safe, and I prayed for our mother, that the kiss tonight was not really a kiss at all. I prayed for the fortune-teller to be wrong, and for her to disappear, to be no more of a real presence than one of the photos on her wall. And I prayed for our father. I would have liked to have him sitting there beside me, his large arms around my shoulders.

"Little Pigeon," he would say. "I'm home."

But it was not our father who I heard shuffling barefoot through the sand, out of the darkness, so that he was first just a shadow, then a shape, and then a man. It was Uncle Edward. He wore a pair of khakis and was bare chested, carrying his shirt and sandals in his hands. And he was not coming from his house or the street, but instead from somewhere down the beach where I had never been, or as I later imagined, from the depths of the ocean itself.

"Pigeon," he said. He did not seem surprised to find me there on the beach, though I was certainly surprised to see him. "Out past your bedtime, aren't you?"

He dropped his things and sat down next to me on the sand, his long legs crossed Indian-style. I could feel his bare arms touch my sleeve, he was so close. And I could smell alcohol on his breath although he did not seem drunk, merely good-natured and warm.

"I couldn't sleep," I said.

I wanted to ask him when he had arrived back home from his travels, and also where he had been to find me so late on the beach alone. Robin no doubt would have asked these questions and many more. But I knew, even then, that people rarely answered questions truthfully. They told Robin only what he wanted to hear, or what they thought he should hear, or they ignored him altogether. I knew that the real answers were only revealed later, after their importance and immediacy were long forgotten.

Uncle Edward looked hard at me, shifted his weight on the sand, then turned towards the direction he had come from—all that could be seen were the outlines of houses built up along the coast. But he touched his fingers to his lips, and raised his eyebrows, as if he had seen someone he knew.

"I have trouble sleeping myself," he said.

I lay my head on his shoulder and he stroked my hair and the back of my neck. We were quiet, listening to the ocean, to the sound of a barking dog, and to each other breathe.

"You must miss your Daddy," Uncle Edward said.

I nodded. The moon was very high in the sky now and I knew it must be very late. Dove would be going to bed soon, or perhaps was already there, wondering where I was, what had become of me. I knew she would do nothing about it, though, at least until morning.

"He should never have left his own children," Uncle Edward said. "That takes a cold heart."

That was not what I wanted to hear, and sensing that, Uncle Edward took me up in his arms.

"We'll find him for you, Pigeon," he said.

"Really?" I said. "You think you can find him."

"Of course," Uncle Edward said. "I travel all over. I meet new people every day. The chances are good."

I wanted to prove to him then that I could help him in the search, that I knew our father was somewhere in San Francisco. Perhaps, just like in the picture postcard, riding the cable cars up and down the steep hills. But I remembered Dove's and Robin's warnings—"Don't blow it. Don't blow it."—and I didn't. I said nothing. My face rubbed against the hair on his chest. He rested his chin on the top of my head.

"You'll be sleeping better soon," he said.

And though I wanted to stay awake, talk with him some more, hear exactly how he would go about finding our father, I discovered I had already become quite sleepy. I pressed my head against him. I closed my eyes.

Memorial Day

Memorial Day commemorated the official opening of the summer season in Uncle Edward's town. The lifeguards would resume duty, all motels and restaurants would open for full service, and resident tags would be sold for five dollars at the City Hall and would be required of all who entered the beach.

"It's not the same in the summer," Uncle Edward warned us.

But that was fine; my brother and sister and I were as primed for change as a carefully tended garden planted and tilled after a long winter. Robin brought home tarot cards and astrology charts to study in preparation for the tourist season. Dove flourished in her job at the restaurant, earning tips far greater than she had imagined.

"Joe says I'm a natural," she told me as she emptied her bulging apron pocket onto my bed; she was justifiably proud. "He says they'll really love me in the summer."

Of course, they would love Dove year-round.

Memorial Day—the words sounded important. Even our mother who had never celebrated a holiday in her life decided she would throw a party.

"A barbecue," she told us. "A summer blast-off barbecue."

She had just returned from work, and rather than showering and going to bed, as usual, she called us all to come down to the kitchen for her announcement.

"We'll throw a party," she said. "A wonderful happy party."

Robin peered at her, then down at me. "I think she's really flipped this time," he whispered, but he was smiling and he squeezed his two hands together.

I, myself, could not believe our sudden good fortune—a party here! Impulsively, I threw my arms around our mother's neck. Her hair smelled of the new cologne she had been using and I wanted to press my face into her hair, feel its softness, breathe in that strong sweet smell. But we were not that kind of family; she would have been flustered, perhaps disturbed. Already she moved imperceptibly away.

"We must get busy," she said, and I let go of my embrace.

"A party," Dove said. She was scratching her fingernail into the table as if she was etching her name, and she did not look up. "You never have parties."

"I do now," mother said.

Since that evening I had first spied on our mother outside, she was doing many things she had never done before. She cashed two entire paychecks and bought new clothes—a white dress with a low neckline, two linen tops, a short skirt, and a lovely turquoise bathing suit.

"I need things to wear to work," she explained to us as she displayed her new clothes out on her bed.

"You could always wear a uniform like me," Dove said.

"And you don't wear a bathing suit to work," said Robin.

"I'd like a dress like that. And the same bathing suit," I said to them.

I would have liked any new clothes. That summer, I often spent time looking through the women's magazines Dove brought home—*Seventeen*, *Mademoiselle*—selecting for myself a new wardrobe from the glossy pages. It was for me the first time I became interested in clothing, in how I looked, and ironically the time I could do the least about it.

Our mother filled a large plastic garbage bag with her old clothes—the loud dresses with their sagging hems, her old frayed pants, and she updated others, sewed on new buttons, repaired a tear. She even began shaving her legs and under her arms, and for the first time tweezed her sand-colored eyebrows so that they arched questioningly upward.

"You look pretty," Robin said to her one evening.

"For Mom," said Dove.

She also took an unexpected interest in decorating. She made teal drapes for the windows in the living room and eyelet curtains for the kitchen, bought prints for the wall, a white cloth for the kitchen table. And she spent almost an entire Saturday dragging me through a furniture showroom in a department store on the mainland. We had to take a bus to get there, and once inside she produced a small notebook from her purse and jotted down furniture styles, stock numbers, and fabric colors. As if she was prepared to buy, as if we could afford any of those fine things.

"You must learn to take an interest in your environment, Pigeon," she lectured that day on the bus ride home, swatch samples stuffed to overflowing in her purse. "Your surroundings not only speak of who you are, but can also provide you with peace of mind, serenity."

I didn't want to listen to her, although when she had first suggested this shopping trip—just the two of us—I had been excited, more amenable. I had pictured us arm in arm, whispering, mother buying me new things, pretty clothes, toys for the beach. Now, though, I was hot and tired and bored, and angry that we had not purchased a single item all day, not even lunch. I stuffed my fingers in my ears, then sucked on my bottom lip, although I knew it never failed to irritate our mother. I stared out the window, and thought of Uncle Edward's still barren house, its emptiness surely a sign of who we were.

"I suppose I'm a piece of linoleum then," I said to our mother. "Just like the floor in Uncle Edward's house."

"You can at least be clean linoleum," mother said, and she spit on her finger and wiped away a smudge of dirt on my chin. I looked up at her, surprised she had even noticed, and felt the spot she had touched, still damp on my face.

It was on that same bus ride home, right before we crossed the bridge to the island, that I caught sight of a man who looked uncannily like my Uncle Edward—the same beautiful red hair, easy stride, broad shoulders. He was with another man, an older man, gray haired, and dressed sharply in a dark suit, bright tie. They were walking together, close so that their shoulders touched, their heads animated as if in conversation.

"There's Uncle Edward," I called out, and pointed through the window for our mother to see. I watched as he pulled something out of his pocket and the two men examined it closely. "It is Uncle Edward," I said again, and then, "What's he doing there? I thought he was away."

Our mother looked, but only for a brief moment before turning inward, her attention focusing again on her purse, on her lap. "That's not Edward," she said dismissively. "It doesn't look like him in the least."

"It is him!" I insisted. Scrambling out of my seat, I headed to the back of the bus to catch yet another look before we were gone.

"Pigeon," mother called, and she reached for me with her free arm.

But I was too quick, and as our bus pulled out around the corner and over the bridge, I watched the two men from the rear window. They had stopped for the moment, and from the distance it certainly appeared as if the tall handsome one was Uncle Edward; he was reaching out now, touching his large hand to the other man's cheek.

"Pigeon," mother said again, and this time she had come up behind me. She placed both her hands on my shoulders, pressing her fingers tight against my collarbone. I could not possibly have escaped, jumped off the bus, run in search of my uncle.

"I know that was him," I said to her.

She shook her head no. "It's dangerous to see everything we imagine," she said to me, but we were both now looking out.

It was high tide, and as the men finally disappeared from view, the water seemed to lap right up to our bus, like waves breaking over the lip of the bridge.

IT WAS in the course of her transformation that our mother had also taken to coming home later and later from work. I often tried to stay awake, to catch her again kissing the man with the mustache; but usually I fell asleep, sometimes even at the window, where I would be found leaning my forehead against the pane when Dove came finally to bed.

"Who do you think is coming?" Dove always asked. "Prince Charming?"

I knew whom mother was with, though. I imagined them together somewhere in the movie theater, perhaps behind the counter where the popcorn was sold, or maybe even up in the balcony, where the floors were stickier, the air heavier, darker. They would be there long after the theater was closed, the projector lighting up only the particles of dust in the air.

Tonight, on the occasion of her announcement, she was home early, though, and she sat with us at the kitchen table, her hair pulled back in a youthful ponytail, her arms freckled and pale. She placed a pad of paper in front of herself, held a pen poised between her fingers. At the top of her tablet it read: Guest List.

"A party," mother said to us again, and this time we all paid rapt attention, took her at her word.

"Like a birthday party?" I said.

"Like a Memorial Day party," she corrected. "Like I had when I was a little girl."

"Were you ever a little girl?" Dove asked.

"Did you ever go to a party?" Robin said.

"Did you know what Memorial Day meant back then?" I said.

I had to admit it was hard to imagine our mother young, like me, not knowing things yet, trying to find out.

Mother ignored us all. "My father was a veteran of the Second World War. He was already too old to be drafted, but he enlisted. That's how strongly he felt about it. Then every Memorial Day he marched through the town carrying a large American flag, and when he saw us he saluted as if we were soldiers. In front of everyone." Mother paused for a moment, then added, "Edward and I would run in the house to hide."

"I know that feeling," Dove said, and the two of them looked at each other with just a fleeting moment of recognition before they both turned away.

"I don't know why we weren't more proud of him," mother finally said. She seemed genuinely puzzled, thoughtful. We had never heard so much about her family before.

"Did he kill anyone?" Robin asked. "In the war?"

"What do you think," Dove said.

"I wasn't asking you," said Robin.

But mother was already busy writing something down, a name perhaps or things to be done before the big day—it was less than two weeks away.

"We will have the party in the evening when I get off work," she rattled on. "We'll have corn on the cob, homemade coleslaw, barbe-cued steaks. It will be fun," she said. "Won't it be fun?"

When we did not immediately respond, she added an incentive— she told us we could each invite one friend.

"That's big of you," Dove said.

"I don't know who to invite," I said. "I don't know anyone."

"I don't think I like parties," said Robin.

But despite ourselves we were all excited. Our mother had never thrown a party before; it was hard not to be excited. None of us dared leave the kitchen table; we huddled together as if awaiting a splendid meal, or plan. Dove started rubbing her arms, looking at no one; she was imagining what she would wear. Robin bit his nails, began making a list of his own. I thought about the very few parties I had been to in my life, of cake and ice cream and streamers. I thought I would invite Uncle Edward to this one. I would want him to be there, and Robin told us he was inviting Edith.

"Edith," I said. "The fortune-teller."

Since our meeting where she had read our palms, I had been having nightmares about her. She took on many forms in these dreams: an old bearded man in one, a talking bed in another, and even our father, although she reminded me not at all of him.

"You can't invite her," I told Robin. "You just can't."

"I'll invite whom I want," he said to me.

"I wouldn't invite anyone," Dove said. "Too embarrassing."

"Suit yourself," mother said.

She told us she was inviting a new friend of hers, a special friend, one who would be the life of the party. She blushed when she said this, a red flush rising from her neck to her forehead as if the room had suddenly grown hot.

"I was awaiting the absolute appropriate time for you all to meet him," she said, turning her pad of paper over, doodling with her pen on its cardboard back, not looking at any of us. "And this will be it," she said.

"A him?" Robin said.

"Oh, man," Dove said, rolling her eyes.

Only I knew whom it was—the man who had kissed our mother that night outside the door. This special friend. We soon were to learn his name was Cary Blair—two first names—and later, when we met him in person, he even instructed us to call him Uncle Cary.

"We already have an uncle," I told him.

"An uncle is one of your parent's brothers," Robin said. "Not merely a friend."

But he would not be dissuaded. "I think the world of my friends," Cary said. "We are all aunts and uncles, brothers and sisters."

"That's called inbreeding," Robin said.

"Get real," said Dove.

It turned out Cary was a frequent customer to the movie theater where our mother worked; that was how she met him. He came at least once a week, and always alone.

"That's pretty suspect, don't you think?" Dove said. "A man always going to the movies alone."

"Maybe he doesn't like sharing his popcorn," I said.

"Maybe he likes to share too much," said Dove, as if she knew.

THERE WAS much preparation for the Memorial Day party. Mother took me food shopping with her, and for the first time I could remember, she allowed me to pick out my favorites—bags of potato chips, powdered lemonade, jumbo-sized peaches, fuzzy and pink. We bought chicken parts and steaks, potatoes for potato salad, cabbage for the coleslaw, and a watermelon that was almost too heavy to be lifted by either of us alone. Together, we walked down the grocery aisles, both of us pushing the cart, me standing in front of her, and she behind, so that her arms brushed the top of my head. We chose decorative paper plates and napkins, miniature American flags on golden sticks, and even balloons.

"Because what is a party without balloons?" mother said.

It sounded nothing like anything she had said before, and I found myself grinning for no reason, then tripping over my feet, so that the cart stopped short. My forehead hit the cold plastic handle, mother's shoes dug into the back of my ankles.

"Pigeon," she barked. "Carry yourself like a lady." But even this was said with less sharpness than usual.

At home we set up the barbecue pit out back, cleaned the house, and opened all the windows. We decorated not only with the balloons and flags, but with fresh flowers, so that mother said the air inside smelled not so much like the sea, but like the sweet scent of the garden she remembered from the house where she had lived as a young girl.

"Edward and I used to have to pull out all the weeds," she told me. "We thought gardening was worse than cleaning toilets."

I was barely listening. "Are you sure Uncle Edward said he'd come," I kept asking her over and over again. I had not spoken to him since that night out on the beach, did not quite trust that our mother had reached him over the phone, exacted his promise (although she assured me she had). I was worried he would not show.

"Yes," mother said to me. "For the hundredth time. Yes. He'll be here."

"How could you have called him?" Robin asked. "How do you know where he is? I thought he was on the road?"

"I called him," mother insisted. "He said a party was a splendid idea."

"That sounds like something he would say," I said.

But still I kept asking, over and over, as if the more times our mother answered yes, the greater the chance of his coming would be. The week before the party I barely slept at all, and even broke out in hives one day for no apparent reason.

"You must have eaten something," mother said as she applied a thick layer of calamine lotion on my itchy arms and chest. "What did you eat?"

"Nothing," I said, scratching furiously, and it was true. I had barely eaten a thing in days.

By the morning of the party, however, Uncle Edward still had not arrived, and I cried into my pillow, unwilling even to get out of bed. Robin and Dove were already dressed and they shouted at me to wake up, but it was easy to ignore them. The sheets were lost at my feet, and my nightgown twisted around my legs. The sun had made a warm bright spot on my cheek and forehead, and a flat triangle across the floor.

From outside the open window I could smell the now familiar odor of ocean in the morning—seaweed, a grounded fish. And I kept hearing the sounds of a child and his mother playing on the beach.

"Mommy," the boy outside shouted at one point, his voice high with emotion. "I've found a perfect shell."

And there followed the sound of his mother clapping, and her delighted squeal in response.

I was envious of their shared joy, and did not want to hear it. I pushed my head further into my pillow.

"He's not coming," I kept saying. "He's not going to show."

"But it's a beautiful sunny day," Robin said, trying to console me. "A perfect day for a party."

I knew it was an effort for him. His own guest, Edith, had turned down his invitation; Memorial Day was one of her busiest times, she'd informed him. A fortune-teller performed a service like a police officer or a doctor—she could not open and close as she so chose.

"Since when do we need Uncle Edward to have a good time," Dove added. "He was never around before."

"We had fun before we even knew him," Robin said, unconvincingly.

But that was all small comfort. A man without food may want only to eat, but after his stomach has been full for a few days, he grows needy and wishful of other things—a cigarette perhaps, a new suit of clothes. Should we ever settle for just the unavoidable necessities?

"I didn't know Uncle Edward existed before," I told them both, clutching my pillow to my chest, feeling its coolness like a balm. "But I do now."

That was as much as I could articulate then, and I burst into a new fit of tears, feeling not so much abandoned, but as if I had been lied to. Mother must not have told Uncle Edward of the party, the phone call had never been made.

"I'll never believe her again," I yelled, loud enough so that I hoped she could hear me.

Dove and Robin continued to console me. "We warned you about her," they told me, as if they were speaking not about our mother, but of an old aunt with bad breath or a dreaded teacher at school. "We've told you what she was like."

"People don't change," Dove said. "Don't be such a baby about it."

"I want to be a baby," I cried.

Still, in the wake of a fresh summer day, even I could not remain bereft forever. After soaking my pillow, driving my brother and sister from the room, I finally got up and dressed. I was not to wear my usual jeans to the party, but a sun dress of Dove's, shortened and taken in, not quite perfect but pretty nonetheless, and I was pleased when I looked in the mirror. I was determined now to enjoy the party whether or not Uncle Edward came, even if Edith the fortune-teller changed her mind at the last minute and arrived with a whole new slew of evil messages designed to scare even the fearless. At the age of five, the prospect of a possible change in routine could turn the day around.

THAT EVENING our mother was jubilant in her new white dress, toasting the summer, good health, and even her father who had served his two years in the war.

"I feel nostalgic for long ago," mother said to no one in particular. "A party always makes me feel that way."

It wasn't much of a party though, at least not the kind I had imagined. The only children besides ourselves were two young neighbors who came over to gape and hustle off with some food; and the guests who did show seemed to not so much mingle as they did to clump together in small isolated groups, whispering, the way we often do in cafeterias, or at funerals.

"Isn't anyone else coming?" Robin asked early on.

"Mother doesn't have friends," Dove said.

"I work all day," mother explained to us. "I don't have time to make chit chat with the neighbors, to grow chummy with the entire town."

"Of course it's quality, not quantity that counts," Robin said with utter sincerity.

"That's what I've always tried to teach you," mother said. She brushed her fingers through Robin's straight hair.

Dove stuck her finger in her mouth, made a gagging sound, and I giggled so loud I hiccupped.

ALL THIS seemed to matter little to our mother. She greeted our few guests with fanfare—her boss at the movie theater and his wife, the people renting houses on either side, Joe Winter and three girls who worked at the restaurant with Dove, and of course, her new friend Cary.

He arrived wearing a seersucker suit and white shoes and he carried a single red rose. He looked a bit younger than our mother did, though perhaps that was only due to the fact that one's mother often appears older than anyone else. And he spoke in a loud booming voice that echoed out to the sea.

He positioned himself in front of the barbecue, slathering sauce over the chicken, stabbing the steaks to test for doneness.

"Here's a hot one for you, Joanie," he said to mother, flipping a steak onto her plate, and they giggled together as if he had told some fine joke.

It was their party, I realized. Not ours. Like husband and wife they linked arms, clinked martini glasses, and argued good-naturedly about what record to play next—Joni Mitchell's high voice singing about lost love, Led Zeppelin shrieking on guitar.

"I've never seen her look quite this happy," Robin said suspiciously. We were not, nor ever had been, children who saw happiness as the natural good grace of life. Instead it was a transient mood, a foreboding sign of what surely lay ahead for those off guard, unprepared.

"I don't like that man," I said. "That man Cary."

Dove passing by, overheard me. "You don't like anyone," she said, and shaking her sleek head, she continued inside to refill her drink.

It was a warm night, the moon high in the sky, and the stars hung over the backyard as if they had been strung there along with the balloons and flags for decoration. In the distance I could hear the sounds from other barbecues, other parties, all down the length of the beach. Children were playing hide and seek, dogs barked as they chased Frisbees, kicking up sand as they ran. A man sang "The Star Spangled Banner" a capella, and his friends and family cheered him on. Behind those sounds, those human sights, were the waves washing rhythmically up on the shore, and the lights from the houses darting like large silver fish over the water.

Close at hand, of course, was our own party, our mother's high pitched voice, ice cubes being dropped into plastic cups, the music playing from inside, filtering through the open windows. I listened to the Mamas and the Papas singing "California Dreamin'" and then the Beatles' "Yellow Submarine."

"We would be warm below the storm in our little hideaway beneath the sea," Ringo sang.

I felt oddly comforted by the words, as if there really were a yellow submarine out there waiting to emerge from the sea, swallowing me up, and then submerging again.

But soon the song changed, another one by the Beatles, "Lucy in the Sky with Diamonds," and not nearly so encouraging.

I was sitting on the porch steps alone—Robin had gone to bring me back some chicken from the grill—when I was approached by one of the neighborhood children.

"Are you living here for good now?" the boy asked me.

He was probably a few years older than I was, although not as old as Robin, and he was wearing a blue Yankees cap and black high-top sneakers. On his knees were two raw scabs, and there was a fine scar running from his ear to just below his chin. His face was covered with freckles.

"My mother told me a whole crowd of freeloaders just moved in next door," he said. "For good."

"We're living with my Uncle Edward," I told the boy. "And we're New Yorkers, not freeloaders." Although I had no idea what freeloaders meant.

The boy laughed at me, and I felt my face burn, my heart pound too quickly.

"I know how to swim," he then said. "In the ocean."

"Where else would you swim," I said.

I kicked up some sand with my foot, looked at my brown bare legs, picked at a mosquito bite. The boy studied me carefully.

"I could teach you, if you don't know how," he said. "My older brother is a life guard."

"My Uncle Edward said he would teach me," I told the boy, although it was a lie.

For some reason this made him laugh again; his laugh sounded like a chicken clucking, but I did not point this out to him. Mother had always taught us if we had nothing good to say we should say nothing at all.

"What's so funny?" I asked instead.

"Your Uncle can't swim," he said, as if I should have known. "He's queer."

"That's what my brother told me. Queer."

I didn't know quite what he meant, nor did I know for sure it wasn't true.

I had never actually seen Uncle Edward in water. "What do you know?" I said though.

"I know a lot," the boy said. "I'm eight."

"Big deal," I said.

He stuck out his middle finger, then leapt from the porch step, landing on both feet, and went to join his sister at our buffet table laden with food. He helped himself to everything.

FROM WHERE I sat I could not smell the ocean, or the flowers, but only the charcoal and the steaks sizzling on the grill. I felt far from the bright familiar beach, as if the house had been picked up, like the house in *The Wizard of Oz*, and dropped not in Munchkin land but in some adult party land where I did not belong. Oblivious, our mother darted like a white moth refilling drinks, kissing strangers on the cheek so that her red lipstick stained the faces of many of our guests. She always returned to Cary's side, however, and I strained to listen to what they said—intimate talk, I imagined. Words that would reveal to me what I needed to know.

At one point I heard our names mentioned. "Robin is dull like his father," mother was saying. "And Dove reminds me of myself when I was her age."

"You must have been a knock-out," said Cary.

Mother blushed, looked pleased. Then she got to me, and I listened closest of all.

"It's Pigeon—my baby," she said, and I could hear every word. "That's who you really have to watch out for. She can be a little spy. And she never lets you get away with anything."

"Not to worry," Cary said and he swung an arm around our mother's shoulders. "I never met a girl I couldn't charm the panties off of."

"Charm has nothing to do with it," mother said.

Cary winked, and the two of them looked at each other, laughed loudly, and kissed.

"They're getting plastered," Robin told me. "Drunk."

"Drunk?" I repeated.

I could see the empty bottles and cups in the trash and even Dove, who was really too young to be drinking, kept returning to Cary, who was acting as unofficial bartender, for a refill.

"You would probably prefer grass," he said to her at one point. "That's what I used to smoke."

"And now you just act stoned without it," Dove said to him.

Joe Winter, in a far corner, stood with his three waitresses, and soon Dove joined him as well. They surrounded him like yapping puppies, but he hardly seemed interested in their attentions. He kept looking over his shoulder, checking his wristwatch for the time, as if he were expecting someone, waiting for the arrival of a new and honored guest.

At one point I heard him ask our mother, "Where's Ed?" and then only minutes later he went and asked the same question of Dove.

"Your uncle?" Joe said. "Where the fuck is he?"

Dove shrugged her perfect shoulders, and for a moment they both looked sad. Then Joe downed two quick glasses of scotch, and polished off nearly a six-pack of beer. Much to our mother's chagrin, he drank them each straight from the can. He ate nothing.

Only Robin and I were solemn and quiet, both of us stood up by our invited guests. We sat next to each other on the porch railing stuffing our mouths with too many potato chips, burping loudly over our Cokes. Occasionally Robin would stab one of the balloons with his pocket knife, but only sometimes did they actually pop, causing startled guests to jump or even drop their plastic glasses to the ground.

"Got them," Robin would say, and I would giggle.

More often, though, the balloon simply petered out, its air whistling as the brightly colored rubber shrank slowly on its string.

"Some wild party," said Robin. I caught him often staring in the direction of Dove and the three girls from work. Although Dove was by far the prettiest, all four of them were dressed alike in short flowered skirts and multi-colored sandals. They flipped their long hair back over their shoulders as if they were swatting at a swarm of flies, and they whispered together in hushed tones. Only once did they look our way, and when they did Robin waved wildly at them, smiling far too wide.

"Cute little guy," one said.

"For a midget," the other replied. And Robin looked back towards the ground.

"Edith was wrong," he said to me dismally.

"She made a prediction?" I said.

Robin ignored me. "Nothing's happening here tonight," he said. "Nothing will ever happen."

"We got to meet Cary," I said. "That happened."

"That's not what I'm waiting for," Robin said, and then, "I don't know what I'm waiting for."

"I'm waiting for them to cut the watermelon," I told him, but I was really waiting for Uncle Edward.

I would wait out that endless party where no one all evening, excepting Robin and Cary, had bothered to say anything kind to me, and only one guest, an elderly woman renting two doors down for the first week, had come up to painfully squeeze my cheek.

"Aren't you just the thing," she had said.

However, it turned out Robin had spoken too soon. Edith the fortune-teller's prediction would come true. Something did happen that night, although it had nothing to do with Uncle Edward. Instead, our final guest turned out to be a complete stranger to both Robin and me, and to nearly everyone else present at the party as well.

He was a young man, dressed handsomely in a crisp white shirt, khaki slacks, brown loafers. His clothes seemed well tailored, yet at the same time as if he were straining at their seams with each breath, bursting out of them much the way Superman in his telephone booth sprang from the conservative suit of Clark Kent. And he reminded me of Superman in other ways as well. He looked like he could do no less than bend steel, see through walls, break women's hearts. And although there was nothing extremely remarkable about his good looks, he seemed as exotic and otherworldly as a movie star or a cartoon hero. This was someone I liked, I thought, as I watched him approach.

On the record player John Sebastian was singing "Do You Believe in Magic?" ". . . how the music can free her whenever it starts . . ." He strode across the yard with purpose. It was not difficult to tell whom he had come there for.

"Stan," Dove said when she saw him, and her eyes shone bright, and then fluttered closed for a moment. "It's Stan."

He said nothing, but swung her around and lifted her off the ground. Robin and I jumped from the railing, our sneakers smacking the sand as we came in closer for a better look.

"Stan," Dove said again, but this time her voice was muffled as he kissed her, the longest, deepest kiss I had ever witnessed in my young life.

Everyone stopped what he or she was doing to stare. Joe Winter, who was closest to the couple, looked particularly grim.

"I haven't been kissed like that since I got out of the service," Cary said too loudly.

"I've never been kissed like that," another man said, and people laughed.

Mother put her drink down on the outdoor table, felt her cheeks with the palms of her hands. Even with her new dress, she looked disheveled; one shoulder was askew, her lipstick had smudged, her hair looked damp. I don't believe she had ever seen Dove kiss a man before. I knew I had not, and I am certain now that our mother, for the first time that evening, felt suddenly old, and perhaps even a bit foolish to be there with her own boyfriend, drinking heavily, flirting for all to see. I saw her whisper something to Cary. He shook his head, and she trembled at his response.

She regained her composure, though, and after straightening her dress and pushing her hair back from her face, mother was finally ready to meet our last guest.

"Can you introduce me, please," she said to Dove in her high tight voice.

We were all surrounding them now, the way children in a play yard surround two brawling bullies. Joe seemed particularly interested.

"A door," I heard him say. "He looks like a huge fucking door."

Stan, however, was unruffled by the attention. He gingerly placed my sister down, took our mother's hand in both of his.

"Stan here," he said, and I was surprised; his voice was deep and low, not loud at all. "Stan Mann."

"Did he say Stan the man?" Robin whispered to me.

"No, Stan Mann," I said, but we could see little difference.

"Are you really Dove's mother?" Stan asked. "You look just like her sister."

"You would say that," mother said, but I could see her examining him closely, wondering about him, her voice softer, more respectful than usual.

"Mother," said Dove. "This is my boyfriend, Stan."

"He doesn't exactly look like a boy to me," I heard Joe Winter say. Then leaning over, he whispered into my sister's ear, loud enough for us all to hear. "You can't be serious," he said. "Guys that size have dicks as small as sausage links."

"I assure you," Dove said. "There is nothing small about him."

One of the waitresses giggled.

"I'm not really a guest," Stan was now explaining to mother. His eyelashes were pale, almost transparent. His face was broad and serene; there was no sense of discomfort about Stan. At Dove's side was where he clearly belonged and he kept gazing at her, then back to our mother, solicitous, polite.

"I didn't mean to crash the party," he apologized. "In fact, I didn't even know a party was scheduled." He laughed a funny short laugh.

"Then what are you doing here?" mother said. "Why have you come?"

Stan ignored her questions. "You have quite a way about you," he said instead. "Forthright and blunt." And then he did something I never saw anyone do; he touched our mother's hand to his lips for a kiss.

Snatching her hand back as if it had been bitten, she continued to stare at him. One could not help but look; he was that compelling.

"I've come for your daughter," he said to her. "She's my girl."

"Your girl," mother said. There was no anger in her words, but a certain recognition, as if she were looking at someone she knew well, rather than someone she had met only moments ago—perhaps her nemesis from high school, or an ex-boss from a job she had left dissatisfied, unhappy. She seemed knocked out, ready for the fall.

"So you are Dove's boyfriend?" mother said.

"I like to think even more than that," said Stan.

"I'm sure you would," mother said.

She placed her hands upon Dove's shoulders and leaned there for a moment. I noticed for the first time that they were both the same height, their eyes the same clear blue.

"Dove," mother said. "You are such a silly silly fool."

I then saw mother's fingers curl into a fist as if she were prepared to punch someone, Dove or Stan, anyone within reach. But no blow was landed. Instead, she ended up merely groping with outstretched hands at the space in front of her, hurling only air at the crowd that had formed. A futile gesture I will never forget, and see always when I think of that night, of Memorial Days for-ever after.

Her face instantly colored as she drew her arms back protec-tively over her chest. On seeing Robin and me, for perhaps the first time all evening, she said, "Shouldn't you two be in bed already? It's terribly late."

Without waiting for our response she went into the house, teetering a bit, and letting the screen door slam conspicuously behind her.

Stan watching, shrugged, and placed one of his large arms around Dove's shoulders. She seemed so small next to him. "Don't worry," he said to her. "I have a way with mothers."

"Yes, we can all see that," said Joe Winter.

Stan ignored the comment. Out loud then and unembarrassed, he quoted a poem for Dove. I thought they were the most beautiful words I had ever heard a man speak to a woman.

"For thy sweet love remembered such wealth brings," said Stan. "That then I scorn to change my state with kings."

Dove smiled upward. "I agree with you," she said. "It's just like that for me."

Then they left, walking arm and arm, so close there was not a space between them, down the beach past the lights of the houses, and into the dark.

No one knew quite what to say next. The night had grown late, but certainly no one was prepared to leave.

"Edith was right," Robin said, and he jumped up, spraying sand with his sneakers. He was happy for the first time all evening. "She came through for me."

"You gotta keep the faith," Cary said.

I sat back down again on the porch railing and thought about Dove kissing Stan.

Was this the man of her letters to New York? Was this love? It had all taken place so fleetingly I had not had a chance to really see what it was all about. I only knew I wanted to be with them down on the beach, walking between them, warm in the crook of their arms. I thought about our mother inside the house, but it was with pity and regret.

"Lighten up, Pigeon," Cary said to me.

He was carrying his suit jacket over his shoulder, an empty glass in his hand. He may have been going into the house to look after our mother; more likely he was on his way home. "You look like the sky is falling," he said.

I rolled my eyes like Dove.

"Kids your age shouldn't have a worry in the world," he went on. "You've got the life."

"I do?" I said.

Then Cary ruffled my hair with his hand. "What a party!" he said.

I watched him go, then rested my head against the porch support, though I was not sleepy, and looked out down the beach, saw nothing, looked back again into our yard. The music had stopped playing, the night had grown quiet. Only a few other guests were still milling around, but they had begun to pick up their belongings, throw napkins, paper plates in the trash, have a last drink. Mostly, however, they looked at the ground or up at the sky. It was as if they were all small children who had just witnessed something they had had no business watching—their own parents making love, a man getting shot.

NOT MUCH later, Robin went inside to bed.

"I need my sleep," he said to me. "Edith and I have a busy week ahead of us."

I said good night, but stayed out on the porch alone. The last of the guests had gone, Stan and Dove had not yet returned, and the night was still warm, darker than ever.

Suddenly from inside the house I heard the sound of music— the Beach Boys singing "Surfin' U.S.A." Then, the back door opened and clicked shut, and mother stepped out onto the porch. She had changed from her white dress into a tee shirt and shorts, and was barefoot. Her hair was pinned back with two barrettes. For a moment, in the dim back light, she looked not much older than Dove, almost like Dove's twin. She stood there, looking out, tapping her foot to the music.

"Mother?" I said.

"I used to listen to the Beach Boys on the radio," she said, although I am not sure she was talking specifically to me. "I imagined I was a California girl. Going surfing with my blond boyfriend. Driving with the top down in a fast car."

"Did you ever go surfing?" I asked her. "Were you ever in California?"

She looked at me, her face open and lucid. Then abruptly, and without answering my questions, she took my hands and with a tug pulled me to my feet.

"Let's dance, little Pigeon," she said, her voice breathless. "Let's dance."

I think we were both equally startled.

"I'll teach you to jitterbug," she said.

And there out on the porch to the Beach Boys' sweet harmonies, we did dance. Our mother twirled me under her arms, swung me around, snapped her fingers, showed me how to move my legs quickly, my body, in rhythm.

"You're a natural," she said as she leaned me back into a dip. My back arched, I felt fluid.

"I am?" I said.

"Every party should have dancing," mother said.

And even after the song had ended, we did not stop, did not let go, did not go back inside.

The Power of Power

Brother Tank preached to a packed house every Thursday night at the Atlantic City Convention Center. He was a Vietnam vet who had established his own religion—the Power of Power, he called it, and he showed people the way to live.

"He has known pain and not only bit the bullet, but swallowed it. And he teaches us that right makes right." This is what our mother first told us about Brother Tank.

She also told us she had finally found someone she could believe in. Every Thursday, which was her night off at the movie theater, she and Cary took the ride in Cary's Ford Mustang, to hear the man speak.

"He has taught me not to ask questions, but to have the answers," mother said on her return one evening. "Being meek and mild is for sheep, not for human beings."

She was always particularly talkative after these visits to Brother Tank, as if it were now her duty to proselytize his teachings to her children. We listened to her attentively, eager to understand the attraction. Robin had done some investigating, though; he informed Dove and me that it cost fifteen dollars for our mother to enter the door of the convention center, and once inside there were further pleas for donations, money to keep the cause going. It was not like mother to spend her money so readily, to give when there was still so little to spare.

"She's really gone off the wall with this one," Dove said. "Stan told me that all these preacher guys are shams. They prey on the unfortunate and the weak."

Dove was always quoting Stan now—"Stan said this. . . . Stan said that." It appeared that everything he told Dove bore repeating, and he said quite a bit. They saw each other most every night, and sometimes even longer. It was not unusual for me to discover Stan sneaking out of the house early in the morning, carrying his shoes in his hands.

I knew they did it in Uncle Edward's room when he was away (Robin had spied on them one night); and once, I woke to find them in Dove's bed right in the same room with me, their bodies silently moving, scuffling up against each other in the dark, Dove's pale fingers clasping the back of Stan's head. They did not see me awake until much later. Stan was beside the bed already putting on his clothes, Dove was sitting with the sheet pulled up to her chin, clutching her knees, smiling. When she saw me, though, she gasped, a small intake of breath, then put her finger up to her mouth swearing me to secrecy.

"A girl couldn't want more than this," she had later told me by way of explanation. "This is love."

"Stan says," Dove continued as she spoke to Robin and me, "that mother has fallen for the oldest trick in the book."

Stan, however, and Dove too, I suppose, were the only ones suspicious of Brother Tank. I, myself, thought he must be an amazing man to hold such power over people, to bring in the large crowds to the convention center, to gain their trust. And Robin, who was usually so cautious and distrustful, merely shrugged his shoulders.

"Maybe it's a need mother has in her life right now," he said.

But it was Cary, the one who not only accompanied our mother to these meetings, but also brought her home, who seemed to sum up Brother Tank's allure most succinctly.

"He is such a charismatic guy," Cary said. "I can really relate to him."

Whatever the reason for our mother attending the meetings though, I particularly enjoyed those Thursday nights. She would come home early from her work at the theater, spirited and flushed like a young girl getting ready for an important date.

While I watched her from her bed, she would take meticulous care in her dress and makeup, sometimes letting me brush her long hair so that the ends lit up with static.

"One hundred strokes," she would say to me. "That's why my hair is so healthy and young looking."

She often would still be getting ready when Cary arrived, and she would command me to let him in, provide him with a drink, make him comfortable. This was not an unpleasant task, for every Thursday night before they left for the convention center, Cary brought us dinner. It was never anything particularly healthy, but this made it all the more appealing. There would be pizza covered with onions and pepperonis, or huge buckets of fried chicken, cheeseburgers dripping with sauce, super size orders of fries from McDonald's, bottles of Coke. Then usually for dessert something he had picked up on the boardwalk—James's salt-water taffy, caramel corn, chunks of marshmallow fudge.

Dove was never home for these meals; she was either still working at Joe's diner or she was with Stan. I knew they went into the city for dinner. She would bring me home matchbooks from restaurants with strange sounding names, and she would speak of tables lit by candles, the hushed voices of other diners, food sampled from each other's fork.

If it were not for the treats Cary brought on Thursday nights I might have been jealous. As it was I thanked my sister, took the matchbooks and hid them away in a box under my bed.

This left just Cary, Robin, and me to eat these dinners, and we did so with relish. Only mother refrained, going to the meetings on an empty stomach. She believed that all processed food sapped you of energy.

"And I certainly need my energy for Brother Tank," she told us. "I need reserves I didn't know existed."

Dove thought Robin and I had sold out for junk food. "All of a sudden you think Cary's Mr. Wonderful," she said to us. "When all he is, is a goddamn delivery boy."

"So, we eat his food," Robin said. "That doesn't mean we like him."

But I remained silent. I knew I was not above bribes. With a box of fudge on my lap or a handful of taffy, I would sit next to Cary during dinner, praise his clothes, laugh at his jokes. These meals seemed to be as close as I was ever going to come to a family gathering, and I did not want to spoil a single moment. I wanted them to last.

"How can such a little thing put away so much pizza," Cary would tease me, or "Just wait until you blossom. You're going to drive the boys wild."

"Oh, please," mother would say, and Robin would shake his head, but they were enjoying themselves too. There are stranger ways of gaining affection than with French fries and candy, and before our mother and Cary left for the evening, I would always give him a big hug and a kiss good-bye.

Aside from these Thursday nights, summer was turning out to be not very different from spring. Despite the heavy tourist trade, I was just as much alone as ever. Robin spent each afternoon at Edith's shop, and Dove and mother were at work.

Of course, the beach was crowded now, and I might have made friends.

When I walked out of Uncle Edward's house and onto the sand, I was instantly surrounded by bodies—mothers wearing large floppy hats, fathers asleep with paperback books covering their faces, children building sand castles, and teenagers of all shapes and sizes lying close to each other, whispering, and more often than not kissing and groping at each other for all to see. It did not matter where I sat. Frisbees whisked past my ears, sand was kicked up as boys raced each other into the surf, the smell of coconut and suntan lotion was strong in the air. And from everywhere on the beach that summer, and from all the open windows as well, came the sound of hundreds of portable radios and tape decks turned up loud, and all of them were playing Bruce Springsteen—"Blinded by the Light," "Thunder Road," and others—but what was most often sung in the streets, or blaring out of passing cars, and all up and down the beach was "Born to Run."

"Tramps like us. Baby we were born to run." I heard the words everywhere I went that summer, and although I wondered at their universal appeal, they had no meaning for me then. The last thing I could understand was running from home, trying to be free. I wanted to be attached, like our mother and Cary and Brother Tank were now attached, like Dove and Stan, even like Robin and Edith. They all had someone grounding them to a place. But out on the beach that summer, surrounded by families and lovers, and so much loud music, I felt as weightless as a loose piece of paper escaping from someone's lunch basket or cooler.

"You always have me," Uncle Edward told me when he was home, though he was not home nearly often enough.

He would escort me out onto the beach in the late afternoons when it was quieter and the sun was lower on the horizon. He would sometimes take me into the water, letting me ride on his back as the waves picked us up and then let us down again, my face protected always by his strong shoulders, broad back, my lips just sipping at the cold salt water, my body feeling the motion of the tides, but not the force.

Often however, Uncle Edward would not take me swimming, but would instead spread out a large blanket for us to sit on right above where the water came up, and he would let me rest my head on his arm. He would do most of the talking, often about his own childhood, which he said had been very lonely and sad. Or about Dove who he said was too much like our mother or about Robin who was like our father.

"Who am I like?" I asked him.

He only shrugged. "You are an individual, Pigeon," he told me. "A girl after my own heart."

I was pleased, but somewhat disappointed at the same time; his answer did not seem to be enough.

Once we even talked about our mother, about her and Cary, but mostly about her and Brother Tank. He spoke to me in his deep melodic voice as if I was an adult, a friend.

"She's always been that way," Uncle Edward told me that afternoon. "Latching onto people who she feels can give her an answer to how to live her life. When she was not much older than you she fell in love with her schoolteacher and camped outside the woman's door for three nights before our father could make her come home. As a teenager she always had pictures of movie stars and singers plastered all over her wall. It was more than just liking them—she wanted to be them. Then she married your father; he was the answer to all her prayers she told us. And now there is this. Brother Tank."

It was strange the way I felt then. I had never before imagined that mother might need someone or something, the way that I did. She was the one who was always telling me how to live—to clean up my room, finish my dinner, stay close to home, go to bed.

"Does Brother Tank have all the answers?" I asked Uncle Edward. "Does he help her?"

"She believes they all help her," Uncle Edward said. "But of course they never do."

Then he fell silent and closed his eyes, and I thought he might have fallen asleep. I placed my fingertips on his eyelids.

"Uncle Edward?" I said.

"Go swimming, Pigeon," he said without opening his eyes, but of course I could not go swimming in the ocean alone. "Build a sand castle," he said.

But I did neither. Instead, I walked back up to the house, changed out of my damp suit, and sat at the window alone, staring out to the sand where he still lay, his arms crossed over his eyes, a towel rolled up beneath his head. Something had angered Uncle Edward, and I tried to think of all that I had said or done, wondered how I might make him happy. He assured me we would have each other forever, but I wasn't always so sure that we did.

I WOULD never have visited Edith's shop again if it had not been for the second postcard we received from our father.

I was home alone when it arrived. I had made myself a large peanut butter sandwich for lunch and was busy licking the peanut butter off the bread when I heard the mailbox lid being opened and then thud shut. There were bills, of course, two letters for Uncle Edward, a clothes catalogue, and then at the bottom I saw the postcard and knew before I even looked who it was from.

Although I had learned to read, I could make out none of our father's sprawling script, but I could look at the stamp which showed a floppy eared puppy, and I could carefully study the picture on the front of the postcard, trying hard to uncover any clues. It was of a huge sparkling lake surrounded by tall buildings: Chicago, I later learned. That was where our father now was—in the middle of the country where the ocean didn't even reach.

All afternoon I sat with the postcard tucked in my pocket; I felt for it frequently and was careful not to crease it, not to bend the edges back. I did not go out to the beach or even to the bathroom for fear I would miss Robin when he first arrived home. I did not go anywhere, but traveled from room to room, looking out the various windows.

I tried hard to remember what our father looked like and discovered my memory was already fading. Instead of my father I kept seeing Uncle Edward, although I knew they could not have looked anything alike. I even saw Stan's face. It seemed to me then that I was losing our father in a completely new and much more permanent way than when he had first walked out of our apartment in New York. I wanted to find him more than ever, and was worried all at once about time, had this vague notion that I was growing older at a much quicker rate than our father could possibly be travelling back home to me.

Later that afternoon, Robin read the postcard to me. "He says he misses us terribly. And he says that the lake in Chicago reminds him somewhat of the ocean and that makes him think of us."

"Does he say he's coming to see us?" I asked. "Does he say he's coming home?"

"It does say 'See you soon,'" Robin told me, but it did not seem to mean the same in our father's postcard as it did when we said it to each other in the morning, before we went about the activities of our days.

"He means it," I said, but it was a question, not a statement.

We were in Robin's room, on his bed, and he turned the postcard over and over, smelled it even, held it up to his cheek, as if it were an item of clothing our father might have once worn.

"We have to find him," I said. "We have to tell him how much we miss him. Perhaps he thinks we've forgotten him." My breath came quicker when I said that. It was too close to the truth.

"There is only one solution to this problem," Robin said. "I know how to find Dad," and bending over he slipped the postcard underneath the mattress of his bed, as if the matter were already solved. "And you mustn't tell anyone about it, Pigeon," he warned me. "Not even Dove."

"We have to tell her," I said. I had never kept a secret from Dove.

"You can't," said Robin. "She won't believe in my idea and it will spoil everything."

I suppose he looked at my face then, saw my doubt. "If you tell Dove about the postcard," Robin said, and he squeezed my upper arm tight in his fist. "I'll tell her you made it all up, just to be mean."

His fingers had made four white marks on the outside of my arm, and I did so want our father's return. Besides, I could not see this latest postcard anymore, and the first one from San Francisco had been hidden as well. It was almost as if I had made them up, the way you can almost taste ice cream on a hot summer day if you think about it long enough, want it enough. I nodded to Robin, I agreed to his plan.

THE VERY next afternoon Robin led me once again to Edith's shop. He promised me that our father could be found in the cards.

"Dad wants to be found," Robin said to Edith and me.

We were sitting at her small table. The room was quiet, and pin holes of light shone through an ill-fitting shade, casting strange shadows on each of our faces. Edith had placed an Out to Lunch sign in the window facing the boardwalk so that we would not be disturbed.

"Only for you, Robin," she had told him as she did so, and he had looked at her as if they shared some secret.

Now, Robin placed our father's latest postcard under a full deck of tarot cards.

"He is leading us to him with these postcards," he said.

It did not surprise me to hear him speak like this, though Robin had always been such a scientific and practical boy. In fact, he spoke like this quite often now, ever since he began spending so much of his time with Edith. Every morning before lunch and then most afternoons as well, he would join her in her boardwalk front shop, and she would teach him what he needed to know. He learned how to lay out the cards, what the various lines in the hands stood for, the astrological significance of our birth signs. He practiced at night when he came home; he took it all quite seriously. If mother had any qualms about Robin spending so much time with this fortune-telling woman, she kept them to herself. She could hardly point a finger at anyone else for being odd, and besides I don't think Robin was one of her concerns that summer.

That afternoon in her shop, seated at her table, Edith told me, "Your brother has the psychic powers."

Although it was hot, she was wearing a long-sleeved blouse and there was a mustard-colored stain on one of the cuffs. She wore sandals that kept slipping off her feet; I heard them click beneath the table, and then the scuff as she eased them back on. There was a gold ring on her finger, but it was not a wedding band. I would not look at her face, though I knew she was looking at me.

"He was born with the gift," she said.

"A gift?" I said.

I thought of birthday presents and packages under a Christmas tree.

"A power," Edith said.

That I knew about, of course. Our mother recited Brother Tank's fifteen tools to power every night to us before bed. "Talk loudly to be heard," was number one. "Get them before they get you," was number six. "Carry a pointed instrument in your pocket," number thirteen.

"What kind of power does he have?" I asked.

I was doing everything I could to avoid her eyes. I examined the lamp in the corner, I watched my brother's pale arms rest for a moment on the table. And of course, I studied again the hundreds of photographs lining the walls, of families complete and whole, half expecting to find my own face in one of the pictures, staring back at me, frightened and determined, both at the same time.

"Your brother can touch a piece of clothing, smell a person's skin and know where they've been, where they are going," Edith continued.

I thought if he could do all that he could surely tell us where our father might be, but I did not say so. "I wouldn't want to touch strange people's clothing or smell them," I said instead.

Edith twisted the ring around her finger, pulled it up to the bump of her knuckle, then down again. "Your brother has a rare and questioning mind. I know," she said. "I have the gift myself."

Robin ignored us. He just kept turning over the cards, one by one, placing them in some pattern on the table that only he could give meaning to.

When at last he spoke, he told us that our father could not return. "Not yet," he said.

Not yet, I thought. That was not what I had come to hear. I had come for a destination, some address where our father sat waiting for us to find him. He would be at the door when we arrived— "What took you so long, Pigeon?" he would say, just before he took me in his arms. He would be so happy and relieved to see me.

"Yes, he can," I said to Robin. "Yes, he can come home," and I thumped the table hard so that the cards just neatly placed and carefully read scattered in all directions, some even flipping onto the floor. "Try reading them now," I dared Robin.

He looked at me solemnly.

"Listen to your brother," Edith said, rapping the back of my hand with a sharp slap, and I flinched in my chair more out of surprise than real pain. "You can't change the cards just by moving them."

"That's not what I was doing," I said, but of course I was.

Robin said nothing as he gathered the cards once again in his hands, stooped to pick up those that had fallen, then looked at me, shook his head, and settled back in his seat. "He can't return until the man usurping his place is gone."

I had not heard that word, *usurping*, before, but I knew instantly what it meant. "Who is doing that?" I said.

"Don't be dim," said Edith.

Even Robin winced, and we walked back to Uncle Edward's, not speaking, both of us disappointed. If I expected something to happen, I knew it was not likely to happen soon. Robin's cards had made no promises.

"The cards read the future. They don't make it," Robin told me that night before bed.

He looked no happier than I did. I believe we both had hoped for more. "The cards give you choices, Pigeon," he said.

But I did not want choices. I wanted a father.

Although Dove and Stan spent most of their time together away from Uncle Edward's, or if at home in the dark after I was already in bed, I did get a chance to see Stan one weekend in late June. It was a rare Saturday that Dove was not working, and he came, with the thousands of others from the city, to spend the day at the beach.

I remember where we all were when he arrived and what we were wearing. The three of us, Dove, Robin and I were sitting on the back porch. We had just finished arguing over who would clean the breakfast dishes, though they had already been sitting in the sink for a few hours and would probably remain there until lunch. Now we were playing a game Dove had made up. Looking out towards the beach, one of us would point out a selected person and the other two would have to tell a story about that person, or give them a name.

"There's Dimple Thighs," Dove said of a woman I had chosen. "And her illegitimate son Albino Face."

"I think he really is an albino," Robin said in a quiet voice.

Robin was in shorts and a tee shirt; he was not going to the beach today, he told us, but to Edith's shop. Saturdays were her busiest days and she appreciated his help. I was wearing the shapeless blue tank suit our mother had bought for me on sale at one of the many used clothing shops that lined the boardwalk. It was hardly flattering, but it was all that I had.

I would have felt worse except that I remembered what Stan had said one night last week when he had come to pick up Dove at the house. I had been wearing the same suit at the time.

"The sun has put roses in your cheeks," he told me. "And a flicker of light in your eyes."

He said it was most becoming, and I had thought for a moment that evening that perhaps he was going to fall in love with me too, that it was possible for a man to love two sisters, even ones as different as Dove and I. Even now, days later, waiting for Stan in my blue suit, I remembered the timbre of his voice, the look in his eyes.

Of course, Dove was truly beautiful. She was in a white bikini, and even though she was pale from spending so much of the summer indoors at the diner, there was a lovely glow to her skin that seemed to reflect the light from the beach. She pulled her hair back with a clip, then, changing her mind, she let it loose again. On the floor next to her sat a portable radio that she had bought with her tips and she leaned back gracefully in the flimsy deck chair and twirled the dial until she found a station she liked—Bruce Springsteen was again singing "Born to Run." She sang along with the music until the song was over, but when I smiled at her she did not smile back but looked angry and also sad.

"If I hear that fucking song again I'm going to smash the radio," she said.

"What's with you?" Robin asked her. "I thought you'd be happy that Stan's coming."

"You would think so," she said.

We had been expecting Stan, but did not hear his car pull up, or a sound in the house, and so were surprised when we saw him at the doorway looking out at us on the porch.

He was dressed in dark slacks, a white shirt, and even a tie, like one of the fathers who arrived on the train each Friday night, but he carried a small duffel bag in his hand which I supposed held his swimming things.

"Hi all," he said. His grin was large, his teeth were very bright. "Smell that salt air," and he tossed his bag of clothes in the air, caught it with one hand. "Isn't this the life."

But before any of us had a chance to reply, Dove was at his side, tugging on his arm. She had jumped out of her chair so quickly that she had knocked over the radio and now it was only playing static.

"Come out to the beach," she said, and she would not let go of him, would not let up.

"I just have to change," he said. "It will only take a moment."

"No, now," Dove said.

He looked down at her, then shrugged at me. "Your sister is quite a persistent lady."

Robin snickered. I picked up the radio, clicked it off.

"Stop laughing," Dove said, and Stan allowed her finally to lead him off the porch and out onto the sand.

He waved to Robin and me once, a large embracing gesture that I took straight to heart, and I saw him bend down onto the sand in his dark dress slacks to take off his shoes and socks. When he rose, he placed them in his duffel bag and brushed his pants off at the knees.

During all this Dove still held onto his arm. She was calling him, coaxing him out onto the beach, where they waded their way through bright blankets and umbrellas, the sunning bodies, as far from us as possible.

THAT NIGHT Dove whispered across the dark room to me.

"I think I'm pregnant," she said.

Stan had left only an hour ago. He had stayed for dinner, along with Cary who had escorted our mother home again from the theater. It had been a noisy meal made up mostly of various leftovers that Dove had managed to bring home from the diner—reheated oyster stew, pot roast, a stale apple cobbler—but mother had made a fresh salad; and besides, it was not the food that any of us was particularly concerned with.

Our mother talked endlessly about Brother Tank. He was going on a national tour soon and was looking for fundraisers. His unusual brand of religion made it easy to be aggressive about raising money; his followers, camped out on the beach and on the board-walk, did everything short of picking people's pockets. They were easy to recognize in their bright orange baseball caps and tee shirts proclaiming Power is Power. Dove had told me that Stan warned her to avoid them at all costs.

"I think I would be good at it," mother told us at dinner. "I'm learning how to finally take what is mine."

"Your mother is a natural," said Cary. "A real natural. If we had had her in the war, we would have won."

Mother beamed. "Brother Tank teaches us we all have hidden strengths.

We need only learn what they are."

It was not until dessert that we learned what Stan did. He taught political science at New York University, and had met Dove at Washington Square Park.

"It was a cold day and she was eating hot chestnuts out of a paper bag," Stan told us. "She threw some to the pigeons, and the others she ate with such grace, such style. I knew right away it was love."

"That's exactly how I felt," Cary said. "When I saw her. Of course it was Joanie here that I saw." And he laughed his strange laugh.

Robin and I chattered too. Robin, about the metaphysical sig-nificance of palm reading. Me, about the purple swimsuit I had seen in a neighborhood shop the other day, and couldn't I please have it. Only Dove was quiet, helping our mother bring food to the table, and then offering to clean up the dishes alone. I should have known something was wrong.

After Stan left, she went straight to our room and got undressed for bed.

Now in the quiet of the night her voice came to me like a gentle tap on my shoulder or a kiss on my cheek.

"I'm going to have a baby," she said as if I might not have known what pregnant meant. "At least I'm pretty sure that I am."

"But you're not married," I said.

"No kidding," she said.

Then I thought I heard her crying, although if she was, it was so softly that it was hard to tell.

"Stan wants to get married," she said, almost in a whisper. "But I can't."

"Don't you want to marry Stan?" I said. I would have married Stan.

"You don't understand," Dove said. "I just can't."

"What are you going to do?" I asked.

I wanted to crawl into bed with her; I had sometimes done that in the past.

She would move over to the edge so that I could fit in next to her, my head close to her face, where I could feel her warm breath, its even comforting sound. But I sensed somehow that I would not be welcome that night, and I curled deeper down below the blankets, tucked my legs up to my chest, wrapped my arms around my shoulders. I could always pretend that I was not alone.

"I guess I'll be a mother," Dove said to me and her voice was muffled through the blanket. "A damn good one," she added. "Don't you think so, Pigeon?"

"The very best," I said, but I think we both could have taken some lessons from Brother Tank. We sounded not at all sure.

In the middle of the night we were awakened by the sound of a loud and excited voice coming from outside the window.

"Who the hell did this to my car?" the voice shouted. "What kind of loony-tune?" It was Cary.

Dove and I leaned out the open window in our nightgowns. From the light of the front porch we could see Cary and our mother. Cary was completely dressed, but mother was in her robe, her long red hair hanging loosely down her back. They were standing together at the curb, and in front of them parked, as usual, was Cary's red Ford Mustang.

We knew he was proud of his car; he had refinished it himself with a paint job and four coats of wax. He had worked for almost a year on the engine and it hummed whenever he and our mother drove away. "Doesn't she purr," he always shouted to us out the car window. I told him I liked the silver horse that rode on the hood, and he had told me it was fast becoming a collector's item.

"If I find the imbecile who did this to my car, I'm going to cut off his balls," screamed Cary.

"That's good," mother said to him. "Get it all out. Use that anger."

"I'll show you how I'm going to use this anger," and he kicked one of his tires with his shoe.

"Cary," mother said, reaching out to him, but he pulled away.

"Dammit," he said, "that hurt," and he held his foot with his hand as he hopped up and down.

It was a funny sight and I laughed, high pitched, without control; and finally, at the unfortunate sound of my own little squeak, he saw us at our bedroom window.

"What are you girls gawking at?" he yelled up to us.

"An absolute fool," Dove replied.

"Go back to sleep," mother said.

"You woke me up," I said. "I was wondering what happened."

Our voices carried out into the dark, and down the block I saw a few lights flick on.

"Yes, tell us what's wrong." Dove said. All trace of the softness with which she had spoken of her pregnancy was gone. It was as if I had dreamed up the conversation. For this was Dove; she never let anything bad or fearful touch her.

"Nothing's wrong," mother said, waving us away from the window. Cary hunched over his car, pressed his face against the door. It was then that we saw what the trouble was about. Across the front and back window of the Mustang someone had written in white spray paint: CARY GO HOME!

"It says Cary go home," I whispered to Dove; I had read it myself.

"I can see that, Pigeon," she said.

"Look at what someone did to my car," Cary said. "I'll never get this fucking paint off. I'll have to put in all new windows."

"Who would want you to go home?" mother said.

"I couldn't imagine," said Dove.

"I'm going to imagine," Cary screamed, and he got into his car, slammed the door, started the engine. But he did not pull away; he sat there instead, staring at the paint and message on his front window, listening to the sound of the car on the quiet street.

"Cut the racket," someone shouted from next door. "It's two A.M."

Our mother merely shrugged, as if troubles were rain that could be shaken off her back. She watched from the curb as Cary sat inside his car, the engine purring like a cat.

I, of course, knew immediately who had done it, who had sprayed *Cary Go Home* on the car windows, and from the unearthly quiet in Robin's room I knew I was right.

"Are you thinking what I'm thinking," Dove whispered to me, her face breaking into a wide grin.

"You bet," I said.

Then we fell into each other's arms and laughed so long and so hard that someone coming into our room and finding us would have thought we were either terribly, terribly happy or, with tears streaming down our faces, very sad.

The Fourth of July

Cary had served two years of active duty in Vietnam and he did not scare easily. He had also learned since the end of the war how to forgive.

"That and a short-lived dope habit were all I did bring home from the war," I had heard him say. And though he quickly learned that Robin was the one who had painted his car windows with "Cary Go Home," he did not hold a grudge.

"How can you just forget?" I heard our mother ask.

And I, who was watching them from the doorway, holding my breath so that I would not make any noise, agreed with her—How could you forget?!

Cary shrugged. "Boys will be boys," he said to our mother. "He was only protecting what he thought was his, what belonged to him." Cary grinned as he said this, that silly toothy grin of his he used far too often.

"I don't belong to anyone," mother said.

"Then I'll just take a small piece of you," said Cary. He took her in his arms and gave her a smacking kiss on her lips, her bottom a squeeze. "I'm just not sure which piece to take."

"Oh, Cary, shhh," mother said, ducking her head into his neck, and giggling.

Red faced, I turned quickly away from the door, and left the two of them alone. Never had I witnessed our father behaving that way with our mother. We were not a demonstrative family. We had been kissed at bedtime certainly (I remembered that), and I had seen our father smooth back our mother's hair with the palm of his hand, or touch her chin or cheek for a moment. But we did not go in for hugging, or that ridiculous patting and squeezing. Or kisses for no particular reason at all.

"There is far too much physical contact in the world as it is," mother had often told us. "Strangers rubbing against you on the street or the subway. Mere acquaintances kissing your cheek, as if it were some unqualified right. I won't have it."

As her children, neither would we. Even as adults, even if we have not seen each other for quite some time, we are all more apt to shake hands upon greeting than those bear hugs some families bestow with such glee. Mere handshakes are met with some fumbling, as if we would rather soon be done with it quickly and with little attention.

Cary was not that way at all. He took great pleasure in touching not only our mother, which he did frequently and with vigor, but all of us three kids as well. He gave us loud smacking kisses hello, grabbed onto our arms or waists if we happened to be nearby, swung me around sometimes as if I were a doll or a stuffed animal. Dove and Robin dismissed him with a shake of their heads, a shrug of their shoulders.

"He's just a pervert," Dove said. "Always trying to cop a feel."

But I could not ignore Cary's attentions so easily. I thought it bothered me when it was going on, made me feel too warm, too close.

"You're always touching me," I sometimes said to him. Or simply, "Leave me alone." But I never actually pushed him away.

It was later, however, after Cary was gone, left for home, that I would remember the warm feel of his arms around my shoulders, or his lips on my cheek. And, instead of bothering me, as I thought it should, I would close my eyes and imagine he was there with me still. Although it was not always him but sometimes our mother or Uncle Edward whom I imagined, or even our father who was giving me the wet kiss or pressing my face up close to his chest.

At any rate, I had learned that Robin's message on Cary's car had not only been ineffectual, but was also quickly forgotten. The windows didn't even have to be replaced but were easily cleaned with a special fluid Cary bought at the auto body shop.

Robin was out with him the next morning scrubbing the glass down.

"What about getting rid of him?" I whispered to Robin when he came in later that day. His hands were red and rough from the cleaning fluid, his face flushed. "What about getting Dad to return?"

"That obviously wasn't the way," said Robin.

Since that incident with Cary's car, however, I noticed that he was making even more of an effort to win us children over. There were still the Thursday night dinners, but in addition to that he began bringing small gifts—a book on astrology for Robin, and small hoop earrings for Dove, which surprisingly she kept and even wore.

There were presents for me as well—a Barbie doll, a deck of special cards for playing Old Maid, a slinky, and my favorite, a silver charm bracelet with a heart attached.

"You'll have to keep adding charms to it," Cary told me. "Until it jingles when you walk."

No one had ever given me jewelry before; I thought it was simply wonderful just as it was. In fact, I loved it so much I was frightened to wear it, as if it would not shine as brightly on my wrist as it did in the small velvet box. I was leaning back on Cary's lap in the living room; the box lay open in the palm of my hand and I moved it to and fro so that the silver heart could catch the light.

"You worried I might take it back," Cary said.

He pretended to snatch at the box, and when I slipped it quickly into my pocket, he threw back his head and roared with laughter.

Mother frowned at us as she had frowned at all of Cary's gifts. "You're spoiling them," she said to him. "Turning them into materialistic consumers." That was one of our mother's most frequently used expressions for evil—materialistic.

Cary slipped me off onto the chair, and rose, putting his arms around mother's waist. "I never believed in that crap," he said to her. "That you can spoil a kid with toys. We always had a ton of junk in my house, and look at how well I turned out."

"Yes, look at you," mother said tearing away from him.

She eyed his pale round face, white white hair, rumpled suit. Then she smoothed invisible wrinkles in her own blouse and skirt. "You have no idea how easily children are corrupted."

But it was not with the same conviction as she had said it in the past. In fact, she had far fewer convictions about us than she had ever had before. Our new possessions were not thrown away. Robin was allowed to continue to see Edith, although mother thought little of her work, Dove to spend her time with Stan. She lectured me not nearly so often.

"I have learned I cannot control you completely," she said to me one evening before bed.

I had neglected to hang up my clothes from the day, and mother, on finding them, had simply left them on the floor without a word, only a sniff of her nose.

"You are a human being, Pigeon, with power of your own." And she sighed, as if it were something for which she still had regrets. She gave me her cool dry kiss good night.

"I am?" I said, looking at mother. She seemed already to be thinking of other things.

It was Brother Tank. He was filling our mother's head with new and strange ideas. She was no longer just a member of his audience, but a real participant in his organization. She had graduated to sitting at the end of the aisle, and at various intervals during the meeting she passed a large silver tray down to the opposite end on which people were to place their donations.

She, also, was to be involved in the biggest fundraiser of the year. It would be held on the Fourth of July in Atlantic City, and mother, dressed in the orange baseball cap and tee shirt of the Power of Power, would scout the beaches and the boardwalk looking for converts, small change, and checks.

"We're even equipped to take Master Charge or Visa," mother told us.

She was excited, as I had never seen her before.

I grew excited with her. Felt my pulse quicken when she showed me the orange tee shirt, squealed when I tried on her cap.

"Get a grip on yourself," mother said.

It was not easy. Unlike other children, I seemed immune to the contagious illnesses that flourished among schools and playgrounds; I was invariably in good health. Instead, I was susceptible to the varying moods of those around me. I picked them up—the highs and lows—as easily as others did the chicken pox or winter colds. I am still that way—with coworkers, friends, lovers. But most of all my family. Our mother's spirit invaded me.

"You'll bring in the most money," I told her that day. "You'll win the prize."

"There is no prize," she patiently explained. "Just the inner strength of having helped out such a worthy cause." Nonetheless, she looked pleased.

I thought for a while that I might even go with her on the Fourth. I could wear my own baseball hat and carry a basket for donations. We could hold hands as we walked the beach, a mother and daughter team. At the end of the day, after we had counted up all the money we had collected together, she would take me in her arms.

"You are a treasure, Pigeon," she would say to me. "I don't know what I would ever do without you." We were a power to be reckoned with.

But like most of the other plans I made on my own that summer, this one too did not come to pass.

"Brother Tank does not allow children to solicit for money," mother said when I asked if I might join her. "He feels it would violate their rights."

Cary shook his head, snorted through his nose. "Get real," he said. "Kids are the pros."

I don't believe Cary ever put quite as much faith in Brother Tank as our mother did. I learned he sometimes fell asleep during the Thursday night meetings, and he had not volunteered to collect money on the Fourth of July, had refused Brother Tank's enlistments.

Mother sometimes said, "Cary is what we call a believer of convenience."

I might have been more disappointed at not going with our mother, particularly since Dove had already told me she was spending the evening with friends at a party down the beach, and we had not seen Uncle Edward in weeks. In fact, I worried sometimes that he, like our father, was gone for good.

Fortunately, Cary made us an offer we couldn't refuse. He told Robin and me he would take us to see the fireworks display that was being held outside the Resorts Casino. Of course, I had heard about it—there were signs posted all over the beach community in red, white, and blue stating 'Celebrate America. The fireworks are coming. Direct from Italy'—but never thought it possible that I would go.

"They're going to be fucking amazing this year," Cary told us. "Be prepared."

I had never seen fireworks before in real life, only on television, and had no idea how one prepared for such an event. I could only lie awake in bed each night, imagining the spectacle, and thanking, of all people, Brother Tank, for my sudden good fortune.

THE FOURTH of July was a black night that seemed forever in coming after a hot slow day. I had spent the morning alone, and the afternoon as well. Mother had been out on the boardwalk early collecting for the Power of Power. Robin was telling fortunes in Edith's shop.

"The Fourth of July crowd is eager and flush," Robin told me. "That's how Edith describes them."

Dove was working at the diner. She had looked particularly pale and tired when she left that morning, and twice she had rushed to the bathroom, locking the door behind her. She ate no breakfast, but stuffed saltine crackers down her throat as she sat at the kitchen table looking old, as if all her youth had gone into creating the baby.

"It is the baby," she told me as she sank onto a chair after her second trip to the toilet. "It's making me sick."

I could easily believe that. The mere thought of having anything strange in my stomach, much less a baby, made me queasy and ill.

My bowl of half-eaten Cheerios sat in the center of the table and Dove picked at it with her fingers. We had said little about the pregnancy since the night she had first told me. I knew she had not yet told our mother or even Robin, but I felt sure she should tell Uncle Edward when he returned home.

He would show her what to do, and I knew now that something did need to be done.

Originally, of course, I had been only too excited about the baby, my niece or nephew. I liked the idea of having someone younger than me in the house, someone that I could take care of, like I took care of my paper dolls, only much better. I would babysit while Dove was at work at the diner, and the baby could sleep in my bed with me at night. I would hold the infant in my arms, tell it bedtime stories, sing songs, assure it that Aunt Pigeon would never never leave it alone. In my dreams I imagined Dove in the next bed, never actually moving away. And oddly, Stan was nowhere to be found at all.

Yet it was growing harder and harder, even for me, to imagine that scenario. Seeing my sister as she was now, and the way she had been the last few days, I realized that the baby would not simply appear in our house one evening ready to be cared for and played with, sung to and fed. Rather, like a terminal illness, the baby would arrive terribly slowly, creeping in quietly, growing far more apparent and serious with each day.

I watched as Dove rose from the table, her uniform neatly pressed, her hair pulled back in a long ponytail. She held her stomach, but it was as flat as ever. No one would imagine there was a baby in there.

"Is it like eating some food you hate?" I asked her. "Like lima beans or liver." I wanted so much to understand.

"Not quite," said Dove, and she leaned over suddenly as if she were going to be sick again right on the kitchen table. Then, composing herself she drew her body up straight, shrugged her shoulders. "But not far off either."

We both smiled.

She closed her eyes for a moment, and when she opened them again they were wet as if she had been crying. She reached across the table with a start, patted my hand.

"I don't know what I would do, Pigeon, if I didn't have you to tell this to," she said.

It was the kindest thing she had ever said to me; it surprised us both. But then, as if reconsidering, she gave a flippant toss of her ponytail, and added, "Not that you're any help at all."

"I could be," I said. I held my breath, felt my face grow warm.

Dove shook her head. "I mean really, I'm talking to a baby about a baby."

Before I could think of what to say, she started to laugh, high-pitched and somewhat hysterical, so that I was at first confused; then laughed too, so hard that milk snorted up my nose, made a terrible sound.

"You're disgusting," Dove said to me. "And babies are disgusting too. They smell of spit-up and dirty diapers."

Strangely this only made us laugh harder, so that my sides hurt and Dove had to run to the bathroom once again.

"This is the worst time of my life," she shouted to me through the closed door.

Hearing her get sick again, I brought into the bathroom a glass of water, a kitchen towel. I sat beside her where she knelt on the floor; she laid her head in my hands. I felt the quickened pulse at her neck.

"You're something else," she said to me, sipped the water, wiped the corners of her mouth.

"You really think so," I said.

"I really do," she said.

Unlike Dove, all I was thinking was that I would always remember that early period of my sister's pregnancy as some of the best times we had ever had together.

After Dove left, I did not go right out to the beach, although it was certainly hot enough. Instead I stayed inside for a while and played a game I had made up when we moved to Uncle Edward's— a game with no rules, no board or dice, only scissors and the catalogues. It had not taken me long to discover Uncle Edward's catalogues; he received hundreds of them a year. Sometimes as many as five a day, and it was only a matter of time before I realized they were good for much more than shopping and browsing, but were perfect for my game of cut-outs. There were catalogues for sports equipment, electronics, videos, adult toys, clothes.

The only ones that interested me, though, were the ones with pictures of people. I studied their faces carefully for my game; you could not just choose a person willy-nilly without consideration for their looks and disposition. For I was creating families and I did not take the responsibility lightly. All sons and daughters needed to look like their parents. They required friends of nearly the same age. Grandparents had to be older, of course, though still sprightly, attractive. And they all needed to share similar coloring and size. I had ten families already, had made clothes for them out of construction paper, and even provided them with pets—dogs and cats clipped from a pet supply firm. And although they were only made of the shiny catalogue paper, their lives were as intricate and involved as any real family's ever were.

Sitting cross-legged, I would prop the cut-out people against my bed or lay them out flat on the floor, enabling me to see them all at once. Like an awesome God, I maintained complete control. I had families torn asunder by divorce and death. Children ran away from home, one mother drowned herself in the ocean, another died in childbirth. The youngest child stole candy from a store, broke all her brother's toys. A father lost his job, beat his wife. Nightmares came alive. I spent countless hours on my bedroom floor playing with these cut-out people, hopeful for their redemption, sensitive to their plights, but never scared. I knew before I put these ten families away for the day, back in the shoebox where I kept them, all their pain would magically disappear. Those who were sick would be cured, the children would return home for dinner, wrongs would be made right, those who had erred would change their ways, all my paper dolls' wishes would eventually come true.

I was well aware, even then, that my game bore little relation to real life, that my people experienced an inordinate amount of suffering, and that even the smallest of family tragedies do not just cease to exist by wishing them gone. Nonetheless, those paper dolls were as close to me as any real person I had known.

Although it was only that one summer that I played the game with any consistency or devotion—the cut-outs were eventually torn or lost—to this day I can still remember all their various names and ages. Where they spent their summers, what their fathers did for a living, their best friends, favorite foods. I think often of the diligent care with which I structured their many lives, and wonder why it is often so difficult for me to care about real life people with the same engagement, the same sincerity of feeling.

ATLANTIC CITY was a swarm of activity as Robin and I drove up with Cary in his red Mustang that evening. The top was down, our hair blown back. My mouth hurt from clenching my teeth so tightly together. I gripped the white vinyl seat, squinted into the wind.

"It looks as if Pigeon is about to pee in her pants," I heard Cary shout over the road noise to Robin. They were together in the front seat, each with one arm slung out the window.

"Don't worry," Robin said. "She always looks nervous like that."

Nervous, I wondered? Is that how I looked? I tried to see my face in the rear-view mirror, but only caught Cary staring back at me.

"You should be nervous," he said to me. "You're off to see some shit-kicking fireworks. And I'm going to see gambling heaven."

Out on the boardwalk we all held hands so as not to get separated in the vast crowd. I could not see the beach, but only a sea of legs as we made our way slowly towards the stands.

"Will I be able to see the fireworks?" I asked Cary.

"They're up in the sky," he assured me. "Even God's going to catch this show tonight."

The bleachers were set up on the boardwalk in front of the large casinos. Cary, who had three tickets, pushed through the fenced-off entrance and helped us make our way up the creaking stands until we found a small space to sit near the top. From up there I felt a sudden panic that I might fall, and then exhilaration as I saw that I was high above the crowds, the beach, with the night sky spread out before me. The air smelled of the crowd, of people who had been in the sun too long, and also of the wares that the vendors hawked—popcorn and hot dogs on a stick, creamsicles and ice cold sodas.

Cary got himself a beer and cotton candy, one for Robin, another for me, and put an arm around each of us.

"The beer is piss-warm," he said after he had taken a long swallow. "But I've got two of the best kids for company." He kissed first Robin, then me, on our sticky cheeks.

"I'm too old to be kissed by a guy," Robin said. "So keep your lips off of me."

"Sure thing," said Cary.

My knees were pulled up to my chest on the short seats of the bleachers, my body barraged by the crowd of people to my left who seemed to move imperceptibly closer and closer to me. I held my cotton candy tightly in my hands, looked out onto the beach where I could see firemen dressed in full regalia waving their arms, shouting orders.

The waves in the distance were white in their floodlights. As it grew darker, the aura of the crowd grew more expectant, as if our collective hearts were beating quicker, our breaths coming in shorter takes. Some man below us began to sing "God Bless America," and others, including Cary, joined in, their voices strong in unison.

As I pulled off a pink tuft of cotton candy from the cone with my fingers, let its sweetness melt on my tongue until it was just a hard drop of sugar, I felt that I had surely never been so happy.

Just as the fireworks were about to begin, however, Cary deserted us. He told us he was only going into the casino for a moment, "to do a little damage at the tables, to get the parking ticket validated," and he would be back before the show was over. Robin shrugged as if it mattered not at all, but I was concerned. How would he find us again in the vast throng of people, how would he even know when the fireworks were over, uncover us in the dark? I imagined Robin and me roaming the boardwalk alone in the night; there was no moon out in the sky, nor stars, just blackness. "Cary," we would shout, and strangers would turn their heads toward us, ominously glaring.

"You'll miss the fireworks," was all that I said, however, and when Cary assured me he would be back for the finale I had no choice but to let him go.

One cannot describe a fireworks exhibition—the noise, although deafening, does not hurt one's ears. The colors are not found in any crayon box. The sight of light breaking up into thousands of sparks in the sky sounds rather ordinary, like a baseball flying through a plate glass window. But there was nothing ordinary about the fireworks I saw in Atlantic City that Fourth of July.

The thousands of people around me fell away, I no longer felt the hard bench of the bleachers nor the empty cone from the cotton candy still clenched in my fist. In fact, while the exhibition was going on, I could not have told you where I was at all. I saw only the sky lit up like a movie depicting war or the end of the world, smelled the ash as it fell, heard only the explosions like bombs rumbling in the earth beneath me. Some of the firecrackers filled up the entire sky, while others fell in hundreds of small individual swirls whistling like grenades as they fell to earth.

It is odd to admit, looking back on that Fourth of July, but I realize it was the first time I understood the strange pleasure of being at once so focused, and also at the same time quite so unaware. When you forget about the people sitting next to you, whether you're hot or cold, whether your legs are tired or your head aches. You forget your body entirely and only see the amazing flair of a firecracker exploding in the dark night.

Later, I would try to relive the sensation over and over; I went to see movies, hid my head in books or schoolwork, tried religion. But even all the recreational drugs I was later to experiment with in college never made me feel remotely in any way as I did that night watching my first fireworks. Charged, I had held my breath; it was all far too powerful to control. Danger avoided, come so near.

And then it was over.

All at once there was the hard bench beneath me, my sticky fingers, Robin nudging me with his elbow. People to the left of me, and above and below me began to stand up, stretch their arms and legs, gather their belongings, start the descent down the bleachers towards the casino, or the boardwalk, or their homes.

"That was incredible," I heard Robin say. His voice seemed to still come from far away. He nudged me again. "Pigeon," he said. "Did you see that last one?"

I nodded, felt for the first time that my right foot had fallen asleep.

"Those were better than I even expected," he continued. "Better than Edith said they would be."

"They sure were," and then I realized, as you do when you discover you've slept through your alarm, missed an important appointment, or a scheduled flight, that Cary had not yet returned.

"Don't worry. Don't worry," Robin assured me as I followed him through the crowds. "I know this area like the palm of my hand." If anyone knew that, it was certainly Robin.

Running almost two steps to his one, we wound our way down the bleachers, then out onto the boardwalk where we slipped under the arms of couples holding hands, knocked against mothers with children, darted among the teenagers travelling in packs. They were busy setting off their own firecrackers now; you would see a lit match, and then in the air or sometimes right near your feet you would hear the sharp pop, like a gunshot in the night.

"We're going to get killed," I said, as I jumped at the sound of another one.

"Killed by a firecracker," Robin said. "That would be a new one. Besides I know where I'm going."

"But where are we going?" I kept asking. My feet felt hot in my sneakers, seeming to melt into the canvas, my tee shirt stuck to my back.

"To the casino, of course," he said, as if we were not too young to be allowed in, as if, in fact, we had been there many times before. Perhaps Robin actually had.

"We're going to find Cary to take us home," he said. And like the responsible older brother he has always been, Robin very directly led the way.

Inside, the casino was an explosion of red and gold and enormous chandeliers hung overhead sparkling in the mirror-covered walls. The smell of cigarette smoke filled the air, and could be seen whispering like shadows under the light. The gaming room was dark and people huddled three deep at tables while waitresses in skimpy outfits resembling ornately spangled swimsuits, and high head pieces, carried trays of drinks deftly through the crowds.

"You kids better hustle along," one of them said to us, but then she was gone.

All around me was a strange sound I had never heard before, could not at first identify—it was loud clinking, soft swishes—it was the sound of money.

Although children were not legally allowed to enter the gambling floor, no one stopped us as we slipped in unnoticed among the heavy Fourth of July crowd.

After the tremendous heat outside, the hair on my arms bristled in the cold air-conditioned room, and I saw Robin and myself reflected over and over again in the mirrors—two disheveled children in baggy jeans looking not so much lost (we would never have wanted to show that), but rather like juvenile patrol guards scouting the grounds, chins thrust out, eyes opened wide, looking at what was magical about this place.

"It's like Disney World," I whispered, although I had never been anywhere remotely like Disney World.

"They like to think so," Robin said grimly. To this day he does not like to gamble, has no humor on the subject at all. I believe it was Edith who ingrained in him that summer that the advent of gambling in Atlantic City took away business, her livelihood. Why seek your fortune in her hole in the wall, when you could do it in a splendid palace?

Still, among that noisy crowd celebrating the birth of our nation, it was easy for me to feel their rush of adrenaline, their tension as the wheel at the roulette table spun around, or the pictures in the slot machine clicked into position—banana, cherry, orange. Men and women kissed each other for luck. Chips were stacked in color-coded piles, dice were thrown, and cards were silently flipped over after the players had all placed their various bets. Although I had no idea how any of the games were actually played, I had a silly giddy feeling inside that if I were to be given chips of my own that night I would most certainly win.

"Lucky Pigeon," all the other players would shout. "She has the golden touch." I would nod and smile as they changed my chips into a large pile of cash.

Suddenly, I was distracted by a loud familiar voice. Louder than the other voices in the room due not so much to its decibel level, but because it was distinctive, familiar to us.

"Hot rolls," the voice shouted. "Hot rolls. Get those hot rolls served here."

It was coming from over at the craps table, raucous, persistent; and when Robin and I looked in that direction we saw to our surprise that it was Joe Winter.

"Hot rolls," he shouted as he flung the dice onto the table, and beside him, leaning closely, was a tall, handsome redheaded man. His hand lay flat on Joe's large back, his fingers touching the jacket collar. It was none other than Uncle Edward.

"Hot rolls served here," Joe called out again, and then after the dice had landed, he whooped a loud, "Yes, that's it. I did it."

Uncle Edward thumped Joe's back, then reached down to collect his own winnings.

"I thought he was out of town on business," Robin whispered to me.

Ignoring him, I asked, "Do you think he's winning a lot of money?"

"I could care less," said Robin.

"I'm sure he'll be home to see us tonight," I said.

Although Uncle Edward had not moved from the table, I could easily picture him soon cashing in his chips, driving home through the busy streets, then rushing up to my bedroom first.

"Good night little Pigeon," he would say. Then dropping a handful of coins onto my pillow, "For you."

"I wouldn't count on it," Robin said.

But I insisted. "Maybe he'll even bring us home." I believed that was something Uncle Edward might do. I had been wondering how we would get home, if Cary would ever reappear.

Robin hissed at me. "That's just like you, Pigeon. You believe the whole world exists just to watch over you, take care of you."

"I do not," I said.

"Grow up," said Robin.

Unnoticed, we watched for a while more. It was easy to see that most of the other men at the table knew Uncle Edward as well. They were older than he, dressed in summer sports jackets, bright ties. They shouted words of encouragement to each other, and at one point one of the men slipped what looked like a wad of bills into Uncle Edward's breast pocket. "Take care of that," he said.

"That's all I do," said Uncle Edward, and the men laughed.

"I don't want to see this anymore," Robin finally said.

"We haven't found Cary yet," I said. But I could tell that we had both lost the incentive for the hunt.

Turning around very quietly, we sneaked out past the bow-tied guards we had passed on the way in, left the gaming room, the casino, and found ourselves once again on the boardwalk on a hot dark Fourth of July night.

OF COURSE, we did manage to get home alone. We simply walked down the boardwalk; we knew if we did that we would not get lost, and although it was a very long way it was not completely unfamiliar. It was growing late, but people were still out, some on the beach sitting among the remains of their parties, stragglers from the fireworks, couples holding each other close, kissing as if they were there alone.

There were only a few people who actually frightened us.

A man dressed in ragged clothing pointed a finger. "I'm going to get you," he said, making me scream, but then he walked on.

Two women dressed in shorts and tall boots came close, their heavily made-up faces looking too bright. Robin told me they were prostitutes, and seeing we were only children, they too strutted away.

Along the way I grew tired, and stopped frequently to rest against the metal bars that separated the boardwalk from the beach. At one point I even whined that I needed to be carried, that I could go no further, and I grabbed Robin around the waist. "Pick me up," I whined. "Pick me up."

But he pulled away. "Shut up. You're not the only one who's tired."

He did hold my hand after that, though, clutching it in his slightly larger one so that our palms stuck wetly together. We walked like that all the way back, down the boardwalk, and then for a while along the beach, until finally we were up on our own porch steps in the friendly light of the entrance foyer.

"I did it," Robin said, still holding my hand, smiling to himself, feeling proud.

"I did it too," I said. "Didn't I?"

Then on discovering the house was still empty—mother and Dove had not yet returned home—Robin escorted me still further, up the stairs, into my summer nightgown, and saw me into my bed.

"You okay, Pigeon?" he asked.

I nodded.

Still, he stood there a moment more. It might not have been out of companionship or warmth, or even to further help me along in the dark. But despite everything else, we were family. And slowly we were realizing that summer that being brother and sister was no small thing at all.

Less than a half-hour later, I was aroused by the sound of Cary's Mustang as it pulled up in front of the house with a roar.

I heard Cary slam the big front door, clump up the stairs, down the hall, and then as light poured across the floor, over my bed and face, he came into my room. He stood a moment rubbing his eyes, saying nothing. When he finally could see me sitting up cross-legged in bed, looking at him as he looked at me, he screamed.

"Pigeon!" His voice was angry and frantic. "Pigeon! What are you doing here?"

"I was sleeping," I said.

"I mean what are you doing here?" he said again.

He came nearer, right up to my bed so that in the light I could see his squinty eyes, his round cheeks, the bristle of his moustache. Bending towards me, he took my shoulders in his hands.

"I was getting ready to call the cops," he said. "I've been looking all over for you. How come you didn't wait for me out on the bleachers?"

"The fireworks were over," said a voice from the hall.

Together, we both turned around; there was Robin, in his pajamas, standing at the doorway to my room. He was not much more than a dark outline in the light from the hallway.

"There was nothing left to see," Robin said.

Letting me go, Cary rubbed his forehead, ran his fingers through his hair, looked back at Robin.

"You really scared the shit out of me," Cary said. "Really had me scared."

"You scared us too," I said. I was thinking of the long walk back.

"It's your fault," said Robin.

Cary threw up his hands. "You guys just don't want to give me a break."

We looked at each other, said nothing.

"Well, it ain't gonna work," Cary said. Shifting on my bed, the mattress creaked from his weight. "Your Mom knows a good thing when she sees it."

"Our mom wouldn't know a good thing if it hit her over the head," said Robin.

He hadn't moved from the doorway. He looked almost frightening, shadowed like that, as if he were actually thinking of hitting our mother over the head.

"Look," Cary said to us both. He caressed my hair now, brushed it from my face, touched my eyelids closed for a moment. "I've never been married. I have no wife, no kids. And I don't particularly want any either."

"Then what are you doing here?" Robin said.

Cary didn't answer him, just looked down at me in the still dark room. "You guys up and left me," he said softer now.

"You left us first," Robin reminded him.

Cary shrugged, took a long breath. "You just flew off, took flight."

After that, we were all silent for a long while, Cary rubbed my shoulders. I thought about what he said. Marriage, kids, leaving, taking flight. It hit me then, and I broke into a wide grin, nearly giggled.

"Took flight," I said. "Like birds, like us," I repeated it for emphasis. "Took flight like birds." I laughed loudly at my own joke.

"That's the worst," Robin said, letting out a moan. He left the doorway, padded away barefoot.

But Cary grinned at me. "I think it's really pretty funny, Pigeon," he said, and he gave me a loud smacking kiss good night, patted me once more, then rose as if to leave the room. Reconsidering however, he bent down once more and whispered very closely in my ear.

"I hate to spoil your joke, though, honey," he said so softly I could barely hear him. "But I never, in all my years, ever saw any damn pigeon actually take flight." Then chuckling to himself, he too was gone.

Expecting a Baby

I have heard that in the sixties they spoke of free love, and equally free living. But little of it seemed to have rubbed off on our mother. There were rules, she taught us, by which we were intended to live, and as we grew we gradually learned what each of these various rules meant—clear your plate before leaving the table, only speak when you have something important to say, never tell a lie, and always of course say please and thank you. There were other rules that were not so easily expressed, they had to do with living a simple life, avoiding extremes, not always following the popular track. The evening our mother learned of Dove's pregnancy I was taught even one more—never never become an unwed mother.

We were all there to witness it that night at dinner around the table. Even Uncle Edward, who had arrived only hours earlier carrying shopping bags filled with food. It was he who had eschewed our mother's grains and rice and nuts.

"These kids need meat. Not that bird food you buy," he said, chuckling at his own small joke.

That night he prepared grilled lamb chops with bright red peppers, fresh corn on the cob from a roadside stand, and warm rolls. It was a more splendid dinner than we had had in a long time and we all felt good-natured at being together. Dove gently teased Robin about crystal balls and told me that my hair looked pretty now that it was growing so long and why didn't I borrow some of her barrettes. Uncle Edward told us stories of his trips to New York—the restaurants he frequented, the off-Broadway shows he saw, the late night clubs that didn't even open until nearly midnight.

"When I'm in New York," Uncle Edward told us, "I'm going to sleep just when you kids are getting up."

"And when do you do your work?" Robin asked.

"Sounds real tough," said Dove.

Uncle Edward grinned. "That's New York City," he said.

He had poured our mother and himself each a drink, a clear thick liquid in a thin-stemmed glass with an olive floating on top, and they clinked their glasses together in a toast.

Just before sipping her drink, mother slipped out the olive with one finger, leaned over the table, and handed it to me to eat. "I know it's your favorite," she whispered conspiratorially.

The windows were open and the kitchen was bright with slats of sunlight and the smell of the sea. The once-bare walls were now covered with movie posters mother had brought home from the theater where she worked—Paul Newman and Robert Redford, Barbara Streisand, Ryan O'Neal—and the counter held my collection of seashells and a teddy bear cookie jar Cary had given to us filled to the brim with chocolate chip cookies and Oreos.

Mother raised her glass to her lips, swallowed. "Yes, New York City," she murmured and looked for a moment like a woman in a movie, mysterious, unknown. "I used to dream about it as a young girl."

"Edith said to dream is to make things happen," said Robin.

"Oh, boy," said Uncle Edward. "That Edith friend of yours has a thin grasp on reality." And at that mother put her drink down and actually laughed, a deep laugh, not at all cynical or bitter.

"We should have dinner like this every night," I said, thinking not just of the food, but of our good spirits, and Uncle Edward; all were making me happy. I had just been about to sample one of the rolls when, at what was surely not the right moment, Dove chose to reveal her secret.

"I'm going to have a baby," she said, just like that, as if she were merely telling us she was going to have another glass of milk. Sensing perhaps that that wasn't enough, she stood up, patted her stomach. "I'm pregnant. With a baby."

For the first time, I thought I could detect the slightest of curves under her white waitress' uniform, although it might have been my imagination. Robin's mouth fell open at the news, Uncle Edward shook his head, pursed his lips together.

"Pregnant with a baby," he said. "What else."

"Dove's going to have a baby. Dove's going to have a baby," I sang with forced good cheer. Robin kicked me under the table. Even Uncle Edward gave me a look.

It was then that our mother heaved forward across the table, picked up the topmost dinner roll from the basket, and with what seemed like great control, wound up, and hurled it at Dove. Without a pause, she then proceeded to throw all the remaining rolls as well, one by one and with great force, not stopping until the basket was empty.

Uncle Edward, Robin, and I watched, but said nothing, as the rolls bounced off of Dove's cheeks, spun on her forehead, careened below her chin while Dove sat there, did not move.

"You stupid stupid girl," mother said when the basket had been emptied.

She crossed her arms in front of her chest, clutched her shoulders with her hands, surveyed the damaged rolls on the floor and scattered on the table, the hush in the kitchen. She looked almost sorry for what she had done, the way the color in her face drained then, the tightness disappeared, and she put her head down on the table as if she were going to cry.

But of course this was our mother; she didn't cry. Instead she banged her forehead three times with a thump.

"How could you do this to me?" she said to Dove, although it might as well have been directed at all of us. "How could you possibly do this to me?"

"Joan, get a grip on yourself," Uncle Edward said. "The girl needs our help."

"It's too late for that," mother said. I could see a small red mark already forming on Dove's forehead, like a birthmark catching the light.

Dove wiped her face with her napkin, took a sip of water. Even pregnant she was still so beautiful it almost hurt me to look at her. She had pinned her red hair back with two silver combs, and her cheeks were pale and smooth, with just a hint of the red marks the rolls had made. She did have eyes like a dove, I thought—shiny, clear and blue—although I don't believe I had ever actually seen a real dove. She stared straight ahead, not at any of us in particular. Her bottom lip protruded just enough to show us how little she cared. Yet even then, with crumbs from the rolls like dandruff on her shoulders, with a baby inside making her sick to her stomach, I would have gladly traded places, no longer been Pigeon the youngest sister, but Dove.

For as long as I could remember I had wanted to be more like her—the utter disregard she held for our family's values and opinions not her own, that mien of complete control. I had often thought there must have been a time, when she was young like me, that disappointing our mother still meant something to her, still hurt. She must have been once afraid of our mother's anger, the way I feared it, and avoided it, trying hard to do right, be good. But Dove rarely showed any trace of humility or fear. Certainly not that night around the dinner table. She merely bit her perfect lips once, swallowed deeply, but that was the only sign that she felt anything at all.

Our mother visibly trembled. "It's that Stan," she said. "I knew it."

"Well, of course," said Uncle Edward.

"I knew he was no good."

"He seems nice to me," I said.

"He seems nice to me too," said Dove.

Uncle Edward tipped back in his chair, rubbed his hands together. "We're going to have to work everything out," he said. "This isn't so terrible."

But the look on his face, his tone of voice, betrayed him. I had never seen Uncle Edward worried before. It made me wonder what kind of monstrous baby our mother and he were expecting.

Still hunched over the table, our mother said, "I can't believe she has done this." And then, "You stupid stupid girl." It had become her refrain.

They spoke to each other now and to Dove, as if Robin and I were no longer present in the room, not because they believed we wouldn't understand or shouldn't hear what was going on—we had certainly been privy to worse. But as if we didn't count, as if ignoring someone could make him or her invisible as well. We heard the hushed words of abortion, marriage, adoption. Words I knew the meaning of, but had never applied to anyone I knew, particularly not to my own sister.

Kneeling down below the table, I began picking up the rolls, putting them all back in the basket. I even bit into one—it was still soft, intact. Robin spread butter on his corn, crunched into it. The lamb chops cooled on their platter. I made sure my napkin stayed on my lap, kept my elbows off the table. Robin asked no questions although I am sure he had many. We did what little we could to restore peace as our mother and Uncle Edward shot their questions at Dove like a splatter of gunfire.

"Has he proposed marriage?" mother asked.

"How old is the boy?" said Uncle Edward. "Does he have any money? Does he have a job?"

"Are you far along? It doesn't seem like you're far along."

Dove sat there, not eating, barely mumbling responses. At one point she raised two slender fingers and touched her lips as if calling for silence. She was thinking her thoughts, although I could only imagine what they were—must everything be so troublesome, so utterly tiring? She listened to our mother, then Uncle Edward, seemed to consider what each of them said. Finally she spoke.

"It's my baby. Don't tell me what to do." Her voice was not angry, only level and cool.

"But Dove," Uncle Edward said. "You've got to be smart."

"You can't marry Stan," mother said.

"You don't have to worry," Dove assured them with a little shake of her head. "I'm not marrying Stan. I've already told him I don't want to get married. He can beg and plead all he wants, he can threaten to never see me again, but I'm too young to settle down with one man for life."

Although she had already told me this, I was again surprised to hear Dove say she wouldn't marry Stan; I had thought she loved Stan. She had certainly seemed to love him. And if you loved someone, wouldn't you want to marry that person, wouldn't you want to stay with that person forever? That's how I thought back then, that's how I thought for many years. But I have not yet married the man I live with although he has asked me many times. It requires an extreme leap of faith to get married, to not only believe that the person will be there for you always, but that you'll be there for him as well. It is a leap I have not yet been able to make. Perhaps I am more like Dove than I ever knew.

"And there isn't going to be an abortion either," Dove told us all. She had stood up again; she looked so clean and neat in her white uniform; her arms were freckled from the sun, her face blushed pink. Pictures I've kept of her from that time don't do her justice, don't show how blameless and unsoiled she always appeared.

"I'm just going to keep the baby," she said.

"You're only sixteen," Uncle Edward said. "You can't keep the baby."

"Will I have to share my room with it?" Robin asked. "When it comes?"

"She's not going to keep the baby under this roof," mother forewarned. "You hear that Dove, you hear that?" And then once again, "You stupid stupid girl."

I sat there sucking on an already eaten ear of corn, feeling as one does when watching a bad magician pull a tablecloth out from under a full place setting of dishes only to fail as the china comes crashing down to the floor. I didn't know why everything had to be so difficult just when it seemed we might all have been happy together. In the shows I watched on TV—*Eight is Enough, The Partridge Family, The Brady Bunch*—our problems would have been solved by now. Our own father, or Uncle Edward at the least, would have given Dove some profoundly wise advice that she would have accepted tearfully. Mother, with words of comfort, would bring in dessert. Robin would eat three portions of pie. And they would fuss around me, the youngest of the family, as if my mere presence was enough to make them glad.

But we were nothing like that. Dove, as pretty as she was, was too defiant; you would never catch her making decorations for the prom, sharing secrets with our mother over a sewing pattern. The brothers on these television shows played baseball or tinkered under cars. None of them, as far as I knew, ever spent their days in a fortune-telling parlor with a woman named Edith. I believed Uncle Edward was wise, and certainly handsome, but he would never be our real father. And our mother was sadly lacking in all the traits that I saw in the calm, reassuring mothers on TV.

I looked over at her now. She had recently cut her hair and it still looked too short, too severe. Her lipstick had dried and caked pink on her lips. She was wearing a bright red blouse and a gold heart around her neck given to her by Cary after their last meeting with Brother Tank. No, she was nothing at all like Mrs. Brady.

She was shouting at Dove. "You get rid of the baby," she ordered. "Or you get out."

"Is that what you want?" Dove said.

"I thought the Power of Power teaches us to all do what we want," Robin interrupted.

He was sitting next to mother and she grabbed the shoulders of his tee shirt and shook him. I thought she might even hit him, but she didn't.

"You shut up," she said instead. "All of you."

Dove rolled her eyes and disobeyed. "You can't just give away your own child," she said.

"Believe me," mother said, "there are many times I would have liked to," and even she seemed shocked at the sound of her own words.

I believe we all fell silent after that, could not bear to speak further what we were all thinking. Mother filled our plates with lamb chops, though they were cold, no longer appetizing. Uncle Edward picked up a magazine and began reading it at the table, Robin pulled out a deck of cards and turned them over, practiced flipping them with one hand, then the other. I concentrated on the food, chewed carefully, looked at Dove, then at our mother, wondering where my loyalties might land, what our father might have said. At one point Robin even offered to read Dove's future in the cards.

"I'll be able to tell you what to do," Robin said. "I'll help you make the right choice."

"Do whatever you want," Dove said. "My mind is made up."

"Edith says the cards can be very reassuring," Robin told her. "I believe that's true."

"I don't need reassurance," Dove said. "Just something to stop the nausea." With that she pushed herself away from the table and hurried into the bathroom; and we listened to what had become, for me at least, the familiar sound of my sister retching into the toilet.

That night, after the table had been cleared, the dishes loaded into the dishwasher, Dove left for work at the diner, and I accompanied Robin to Edith's. Under normal circumstances our mother would have said it was too late for us to go out, but this had not been a normal night. She and Uncle Edward had retired to the living room and I could hear them bickering, mother's voice sharp and high, Uncle Edward's deep clipped tones.

"You knew she was sleeping with him, Joan," we heard Uncle Edward say at one point. "What did you expect?"

"I don't know," mother said. "But not this. She's only a little girl. She's my little girl."

Robin and I, peering from the kitchen, watched as she let her face drop against the side of the couch. Later, before we left, Uncle Edward took my hand and touched it to his lips.

"Don't worry, little Pigeon," he said. "This is really just a drop in the ocean."

He kissed me and held me close for a moment. Our mother only nodded good-bye.

I DIDN'T go into Edith's with Robin that night, but instead stood outside of her shop on the boardwalk. Although somewhat frightened to be by myself, I was more frightened of what might lie inside. The dark table, the well worn cards. I didn't want all those photographs of the smiling people staring at me from the walls either, poking fun at my sad family. And I didn't want Edith pointing her long finger across the vague lines in my palm, accusing me somehow of causing Dove's pregnancy, or at the very least causing her unhappiness. It didn't matter that I knew generally how babies were conceived and born; Dove had filled me in early. There was still enough mystery surrounding the procedure that I thought it possible I could be blamed, that Edith could find some reasonable explanation.

Now, as an adult, with even more knowledge, I still have that same tendency to blame myself for other's misfortunes—my friend's, my lover's. I listen to their troubles, give advice, explore various paths they might take, and like a priest hearing confession, find some way to absolve us both from guilt. As if I held some control over their lives.

Or as Edith might have said, I believed I could pick and choose where each tarot card might fall.

ROBIN HAD already warned me: If I were not coming in with him, I was also not to leave the spot outside Edith's shop.

"You just stay right there," he said, as if I was some trained dog. Just before entering himself, he placed his face close to mine. "I'll find out what Dove should do. I'll find the answer." His face looked so earnest and so old, I believed he might just do that.

After he was gone, I leaned against Edith's door for a while, and growing tired of that I sat down on the planks of the board-walk. I put my arms around my bare legs, held my knees close to my body, breathed in the salt and shampoo smell of my hair. Although late, it was summer and still light out, but from that low position I could not see the ocean or the casinos. I saw moving wheels, pedals, people.

It was the time of night that the boardwalk was open for bicycle riders, and it seemed like hundreds of them passed me while I sat, creating breezes as they rolled by. There were couples on tandems, old men with baskets in the front of their thick-tired bikes, boys wearing black tights hunched over their handlebars, and whole families riding together. Fathers and mothers with seats on the back of their bikes for toddlers, and their children on smaller bicycles behind them, beeping their horns, ringing their bells. I would have liked to be riding along with them, but I didn't know how to ride a bicycle, didn't even own one. No one in my family did.

Suddenly from just above me, I heard someone call out my name. When I looked up I saw my neighbor, the boy with the freckles and baseball cap who had crashed our Memorial Day party. He had stopped his bike in front of me; it was a beautiful one, bright red with long streamers hanging down from each handlebar, and a bell and a horn—and he straddled the center bar.

"Hi, Pigeon," he said again. "What are you doing here?"

I had seen him a few times since that first party of the summer, on the beach, or eating with his family at the picnic table they had set out on their back deck. I had even learned his name; it was Tom. But we had never really spoken again. I still remembered what he had said about my Uncle Edward, what he had inferred about me.

"I asked you what you're doing here." he said again.

"I'm sitting," I said. "Can't you see?"

"All by yourself?" he asked.

Just a few shops up the boardwalk I could see the rest of his family, his parents, his older sister and brother. They were all strad-dling their bright shiny bikes, just like Tom, while their father bought them ice-cream cones at the stand.

"Yes, all by myself. I do lots of things by myself." I said it as if it were a badge of honor, although it rarely felt that way to me.

He scuffed the toe of his sneaker against the wood, considered what I had said.

"I guess you think you're pretty cool." He looked at me directly face on for the first time. His freckles seemed to have gotten more plentiful since the beginning of the summer, his scar had deepened.

"I don't know," I said. I really didn't.

"Well, my mom said if you want to come over some time, you can."

I looked over at his family again; they were all licking their ice-cream cones now and his brother was waving for Tom to come and join them.

I looked at his mother. She was overweight and she wore pink sneakers and pale pink shorts and a matching kerchief around her hair. She leaned over her handlebars licking her ice-cream cone neatly from bottom to top; and although I could see she was talking to her husband, and her children, I could not hear what she was saying. She did have a kind face and I would have liked to meet her, meet Tom's father too, but I couldn't imagine myself actually going over to their house, sitting in their kitchen or on their deck, even if it was only next door. I was not sure my mother would have approved.

"I don't know," I said to Tom. I held my hair back with one hand, peered up at him. "I'll see."

"Suit yourself," he said.

Kicking off with his high-top sneaker, he jumped up on his bike and rode off to claim his ice-cream cone.

I felt a bit lonely after he was gone, and also chilled, although it was still hot outside. It was starting to get dark and the boardwalk thinned out of bicycles and families; in their place came the casino patrons.

Unlike the bikers, they were not dressed for the beach but for the evening. Men with jackets slung over their shoulders, women in bright-colored outfits and high-heeled shoes stumbling occasionally on the cracks in the boards. They were coming and going from one casino to the other, trying out their luck, sometimes stopping along the way to buy a hot dog from the vendor or a box of salt water taffy or fudge to take home as a souvenir. One woman, with piled high brown hair and a low-cut yellow blouse, even pulled her companion over to Edith's shop where I sat.

"Harry, I want my fortune told," she said in a high-pitched voice.

"I'll tell you your fortune," he said laughing, but then reaching into his pocket he pulled out some bills and handed them to the woman. "Go ahead," he said. "Have her tell you where we should play next."

"I'll do just that, Harry," she said and she kissed him loudly on the lips. Then looking down at me for the first time, she smiled and patted my head. "Hi, dearie," she said. "Don't you think it's about time for you to be getting home. Isn't your mommy worried about you?"

But she had disappeared inside the door before I could even answer.

When Robin finally came out, he did not look happy. "Let's go home," he said to me, and he took my arm and pulled me to my feet. "Now."

"What did she say?" I asked as he pulled me along down the boardwalk. "What should Dove do?"

Robin shook his head, kept walking. "The cards were pretty confusing," he finally admitted.

"But what does Edith think?" I said.

I thought it surprising that he had not already told me; he was always quoting Edith. I wondered if it was too terrible for even Robin to repeat.

"Edith doesn't come right out and tell you what to do," Robin said.

He had stopped for a moment to tie his shoelace. As he bent over, I could see that his ears were very red, from the sun or embarrassment. When he stood up again, he shrugged his shoulders. "I don't know. Edith thinks Dove is an idiot, to get pregnant like that. She knew it was going to happen."

"She did?" I said.

"Edith thinks if Dove is smart she'll marry Stan. Give the baby a father, if she's smart."

"Is that all?" I said.

But as we grew closer and closer to home I feared that Dove was not particularly smart in the way that Edith meant her to be. Dove was the kind of girl who could confuse the tarot cards and fortune tellers, behave like a grown woman at sixteen, make our mother almost break down and cry.

I remembered her coming into our bedroom that night as if it were a dream. I did not know what time it was, only that it was far later than Dove normally returned from the diner, and her hair, which was always neatly pinned back, was now down and tangled. In the dark I watched from my bed as she pulled her white and yellow uniform over her head, let it fall to the floor, and then instead of putting on her nightgown changed into her bathing suit and slipped a tee shirt on over that. I think she knew I was watching her, but she said nothing, did not acknowledge me at all. When she left the room, I could not hear her footsteps, but imagined her barefoot going down the stairs and then out the back door, where she quietly let the screen close behind her.

I wondered if she had gone to meet Stan, although she had already told me that Stan had refused to see her since she had turned down his proposal of marriage. I wondered even if she had gone off to have the baby all alone in the night.

It did not take me long to follow her. Robin and mother were long asleep, and Uncle Edward's car was gone and could not be expected back quickly, so I had little fear of getting caught. I did not even bother to change out of my summer nightgown, but crept quietly out onto the back porch and barefoot onto the beach.

I did not see Dove right away. The sand appeared deserted and the nearby houses were dark. Only the casino lights were bright in the sky, beckoning from the distance. It was high tide and there was little beach to walk upon. When the waves broke I felt the cool water slide across my feet, sometimes rising to my ankles, and the crunch of broken shells under my toes.

Then I saw her.

At first I thought she was just lying on the water, but then I saw she had Uncle Edward's float—a white Styrofoam board—and she lay on it the way the surfers did as they waited for a perfect wave. As the waves came they lifted her up so that her body slanted backward and I could see only her head and her hands, and then she was again let down and I could see all of her, her face, her bare shoulders, her body stretched out on the surf. Although she was a strong swimmer and not far out, although the water was quite calm that night, still I feared for her out there in the ocean.

"Dove," I called to her. "Come in. Come in."

At first she didn't hear me, and I waded further into the water so that the bottom of my nightgown grew wet and heavy, and I called again. "Come in. Come in."

I thought I sounded like a sea gull, high and urgent, and perhaps Dove would pay me no mind. But when I shouted to her a third time, she looked up and with the next big wave, she began paddling, and when it rose she let it pick her up and take her to shore, where she skimmed along the surf before finally landing not far from where I stood.

"Are you okay?" I said.

"What do you think," she said.

She lay there for a moment breathing heavily, her tee shirt clinging wetly to her suit. Then she picked up Uncle Edward's board under one arm and pulled me along with the other.

"What are you doing out here in your pajamas anyway," she said to me.

"Get inside and go to bed."

"I don't have to listen to you," I said spitefully.

"Of course you do. I'm your big sister."

After which she gave a quick tug to my hair, chased me on up the beach, and together we tiptoed back into the house.

THE NEXT morning Uncle Edward presented us with a third postcard from our father.

"Look what came in the mail," he said, stepping out onto the back porch where I sat with Dove. Robin had already left for Edith's, and mother was inside the house getting ready for work. Dove, who was not yet dressed, lay stretched out on her back; she did not even look up at Uncle Edward's announcement.

But I did. I thought for a moment he might have another catalogue for me; he knew I collected them. But when I saw the small card in his hand I knew exactly what it was.

"It's from Daddy," I shrieked, leaping up to retrieve it from him.

He was not so willing to let it go, however, and dangled it in the air above my head where I could not quite reach it.

"Try to get it," he said in a teasing voice. "Get it," before finally letting it loose so that it fluttered for a moment in the breeze.

I caught it, and held it close before inspecting it as if I feared it might suddenly escape from my hands and float away.

It was from our father and he was close by. On the front was a picture of the Statue of Liberty in bright neon colors superimposed next to the Empire State Building.

"I'm in New York," it said on the back. "And I'll be home for Pigeon's birthday. I miss you all."

"The Big Apple," Uncle Edward said.

"Whoopee," said Dove from the floor.

I was busy trying to figure out how many weeks, days, even hours it was until my next birthday. I counted on my fingers, got lost, recounted.

"So your dad has come back to nest," Uncle Edward said. He peered over my shoulder at the card, examined the stamp and its cancellation mark.

"My birthday is not until September," I said, with the realization that a lot could still happen before my birthday rolled around.

Uncle Edward had never been around for my birthday before; he might not have known.

"That's a long time away," I said.

"What do you expect," Dove said.

I shrugged. "Why would he wait so long?"

Dove's nightgown flittered transparently up with each small gust of wind and she did little to try to hold it down. Her outstretched legs were tan and smooth, and I noticed that she had painted each of her toenails a bright shocking pink. Around her right ankle was a thin gold chain I had never seen before; if she had been wearing it last night in the water I had not noticed. Instead of sitting up to see the card, she closed her eyes.

"Grow up, Pigeon," she said. "Figure it out. Daddy is not coming back."

"What about the postcards?" I said.

But by this time, even for me, the postcards from our father, our father himself, had taken on an unreal quality.

I do not believe it was because we missed him any less. I knew a day did not go by that I didn't think of him. Perhaps not as clearly as I might have liked—I no longer remembered the color of his eyes, the shape of his face, the scent of his clothes—but at the very least I always retained a hazy imprecise view of what our father meant to me, who he was. And I knew I suffered his loss.

"He is too coming back," I shouted at Dove. "He said so."

Yet it was also true my birthday was a long way off, or so it seemed to me, and by then he might have left New York City altogether, gone to another state. There he would purchase a new picture postcard in the local gas station and send it to us here, care of Uncle Edward. Utah, the card might say, at the Great Salt Lake, or Texas on the border. It was too terrible to think of and I began to cry, so hard that my eyes stung, my chest hurt, tears dripped from my nose onto the postcard, making water marks on the lights of the Empire State Building.

Uncle Edward knelt down beside me, pulled me into his arms, tried to comfort me. "Pigeon," he said. "Please don't cry."

"But I want my father," I sobbed.

"Don't cry," he said again. "We have each other."

"Through thick and thin," Dove intoned from the floor. "Whether pregnant or virgin."

"I'm here for you."

Dove gave a snort of disgust through her nose. "You really stood by me at dinner. You really showed me you cared."

I believe she got to him then, as well as if she had actually risen up and smacked him across the face. He tapped his chin a few times with the front of his fist, he bit a nail. When he finally regained his composure, he picked me up onto his lap where I could look into his face.

"I'll tell you what we can do, little Pigeon," he said in his soft deep voice. I could see even Dove perk up to hear what he might suggest.

"I have to be in New York on business next week," he said. "Why don't you come with me and we'll do something fun together. We can go to a museum and see suits of armor, or to the planetarium and see a million stars."

"You mean you'll take me with you?" I asked.

"You bet," Uncle Edward said.

"Oh, really," Dove said shaking her head, snickering. "Go to New York. Now that's a perfect solution."

She gathered herself up, swirling her hair back from her face with a vigorous shake of her head, and stared at Uncle Edward with a look I had thought until then she had reserved only for our mother.

"In fact, maybe you'll find Daddy in New York," she said, sarcastically.

"Maybe we just will," I said.

She rolled her eyes. "I'm going inside."

Before doing so, however, she stooped next to me, and as quickly as a pickpocket palms a man's wallet, she snatched our father's postcard away.

"Hey," I said. "Give that back."

But she had already disappeared with it into the house, letting the screen door bounce shut behind her.

"Pregnant women are notorious for their moods," Uncle Edward said when she was gone, but not really to me.

He was still holding me, and I rubbed my hand up and down the red hair on his arms, laid my head on his chest.

It was then that an idea hatched in my mind. I suddenly could only connect our trip to New York with a search of my own—to find our father. I knew Dove would tell me I was too little, or too afraid, or perhaps just too stupid to find our father. But I would prove her wrong. I didn't need Robin's tarot cards, or Dove's bravery. I needed only a ride to where our father was to make us all whole again, to restore what used to be ours.

"Are we really going to New York?" I asked Uncle Edward, just to make sure he would not change his mind. "Will you really take me?"

"Of course I will," Uncle Edward said to me, and he stroked my hair. "We'll have a wonderful time."

I wanted to tell him I didn't need suits of armor or a building full of stars to have a good time—I needed only to be where our father was living. I thought about him singing his song about the pigeon to me at night and how it felt so good. I would find him; he was right in our own hometown, it would be easy. He might even be out looking for me.

THE FOLLOWING Thursday night Cary came with four large bags from McDonald's under his arm. He was also fairly bursting with news.

"Guess what I just saw?" he said as he placed the bags onto the kitchen table, tossed his keys onto the countertop, let me leap into his arms.

I had been ready for him. Robin and I had both been waiting, heard his car pull up in front of the house, were there to greet him and hear what it was he had to say.

"What did you see?" I said.

Robin rifled through the bags, pulling out a cardboard cup of French fries, a Styrofoam container holding a Big Mac, and still standing, began stuffing fries into his mouth.

"We're not barbarians, are we?" our mother said to him as she approached from the doorway. "Use a plate and fork, and wait for the rest of us to sit down."

She was already dressed for her Power of Power meeting, and looked almost pretty, almost young, in a flowered cotton jumper, a white blouse. She pushed her short red hair behind her ears, and even through her annoyance at Robin, I saw something in mother's face that might have passed for pleasure at Cary's arrival. Perhaps under other circumstances I wouldn't have even noticed her attractiveness, but she had already agreed that Uncle Edward could take me to New York next week when he went. For one night only, but I could go. And since then, I had been looking at her with far greater sympathy and forgiveness.

"Doesn't anyone want to hear my news?" Cary said, fairly shouting now. "Don't you want to know what I saw?"

"I do," I said. I was hanging onto his arm and he swung me around like a marionette.

"We all do," mother said.

Circling me, she went and kissed him dryly on the cheek.

Cary let me go then, crossed his arms in front of his chest, rocked back and forth in his shoes. "Guess whose name is painted in the brightest biggest letters across the side wall of the diner?"

He said it as if it were something we all wanted to hear, but I gathered almost immediately that it was not.

"I couldn't begin to guess," mother said, but I think she had a good idea. She sat down suddenly as if she had all at once grown tired.

Robin, who had finished setting the table, sat down in his chair beside our mother. He stuffed a few more fries in his mouth, stared pointedly at Cary.

"Well, are you going to tell us or do you want us to torture it out of you?"

"Whose name?" I said.

"Dove's," Cary said in a final expulsion of breath. "And not alone either."

"Someone wrote 'Joe Loves Dove' in bright red spray paint across the outside wall of the diner. 'Joe Loves Dove' almost six feet high." He was fairly beaming.

"Who's this Joe?" mother asked.

Through sheer habit she began emptying the paper bags, placing an unidentified Styrofoam container at each of our plates, although no one but she and Robin were sitting down, and none of us were interested in food now. "Joe who?"

"Joe Winter," I said; it was obvious.

"That would be my guess," Cary said.

Mother frowned. "With Dove?" she said. "Joe Winter must be well over thirty years old. He couldn't possibly be in love with her."

"Age has nothing to do with it, my dear," Cary said.

Our mother seemed not to listen; she picked out one French fry, ate it, made a face, pushed the rest of the food away. She had long warned us of the dangers of junk food although we barely listened, told us how it would clog our arteries, make us old before our time.

"Do you know who did it?" Robin asked Cary.

"Who would do such a terrible thing?" mother said. "Defacing public property."

"Someone in love," Cary grinned.

"Maybe Stan," I guessed.

Mother glared at me.

"Maybe Joe Winter, trying to drum up business," Robin suggested.

"Maybe it's not our Dove at all," mother said.

"Oh, sure," Cary said. He came up behind her, put his arms around her neck, kissed the nape. "The whole town is just filled with girls named Dove."

"I just don't believe it's our Dove," mother said quite firmly.

"I wouldn't bet the ranch," Cary said.

I knew then that Cary did not yet know about Dove, about her pregnancy. Perhaps our mother was planning on telling him tonight, or perhaps not at all. He would discover as a stranger might, as

Dove's stomach swelled so that it was obvious to anyone that she was not merely gaining weight, but was carrying a baby inside. Then a second glance at her left hand would reveal there was no wedding band, no husband.

"Joe Loves Dove," I said. "Do you think he really does?"

"I think stranger things have happened," Cary said.

"I think we should all sit down and eat," mother said. It was not just a thought, but a command, and all of us obeyed.

I pulled the pickles and onions off my hamburger, pushed them to the side of my plate, scraped at the ketchup and mustard, took a bite. I looked over at Robin and Cary, who were each taking huge messy bites out of their own burgers, holding them with both hands. Only mother wasn't eating. Nor had she eaten much since she had learned of Dove's pregnancy. And she had missed two nights of work as well.

"I just can't face the movies," she said to me, as if that justified everything. But I could understand; the movies, like television, all must have seemed rather pointless to our mother, in a world that was growing increasingly complex.

She had been planning, however, on attending the meeting that evening with Cary.

"It will give me energy," she had told me earlier in the day. "Brother Tank will show me what to do."

Now, with this latest bit of news, it looked like she would forego even that. With one hand she untied the scarf around her neck, twisted it around her fist as if it were a bandage, untwisted it, left it in a small heap on the table. I could see the blue veins at her temple, the tautness of her neck.

"I could show it to you, Joan, on the drive over tonight," Cary suggested to her. "There was a whole crowd gathered earlier. They're all placing bets on who did it. Or we could even go in and ask Dove herself. Doesn't she work there tonight?"

"Can I come too?" Robin said. "I think I could come up with who did it."

"Really," mother said. With that, she seemed to change her mind about the course of the evening; she rose from her chair, pushed it quickly in. "We're going to see Brother Tank," she commanded. "Not any side show attractions."

"Some might call Brother Tank a side show attraction," Cary said, still chuckling.

"Then they would be missing the entire point. People without trust or faith."

She retied her scarf around her neck, patted her cheeks, retrieved her purse from where she kept it near the door. It would take someone far less bright than Cary not to see that our mother was ready to leave.

He left his own dinner half eaten, rose quickly to join her at the door. And it would take a child even younger than me not to know that our mother was a believer. Even in the midst of what for years she called her own personal tragedy, she was filled with trust for Brother Tank, and faith that he could somehow some way help her put things finally to right.

Searching New York City

It hadn't felt really hot all summer until I sat in that air-conditioned apartment in New York. It was what was called central air conditioning (something I had not yet experienced in my young life); the cool air was forced through vents in the floor, causing the blinds to vibrate, the plant leaves to flutter as if caught in a breeze. A low-intensity hum filled the room. Yet despite all these signs of a cooler climate, I sat perspiring on an oversized leather couch and I imagined myself, among the fronds of the large plants, caught in a tropical heat wave.

We had arrived by car less than an hour before. The apartment belonged to a man named Rick who was a friend of Uncle Edward's. He spoke in strange clipped tones and cocked his head in my direction several times, as if to say "Is that her? Is that really her?"

Almost immediately upon our arrival, he related to Uncle Edward a story about an acquaintance of theirs, a man who had swallowed almost half a box of Cascade dishwasher detergent.

"The more water we gave him the more that soap activated within his stomach."

Uncle Edward raised his eyebrows, looked over at me, and Rick took in his breath quickly.

"Well he died," Rick finished up.

"He passed away," said Uncle Edward. "Went to a better place."

"If you consider a hospital morgue a better place," Rick said.

I could not imagine why anyone would eat dishwashing detergent; it must have tasted terrible, but I could see the poor man with soap bubbling not only out of his mouth, but out of his ears and nose and eyes as well. It was a sorry and scary sight.

"That's disgusting," I said.

"The man was dying anyway," Uncle Edward reassured me.

"Of a broken heart," said Rick.

That I could certainly understand; it seemed to me we were often all in danger of dying of broken hearts.

Rick spoke also of a woman named Magda who was giving a great new show, and a new restaurant that allowed diners to help prepare their own meals table-side.

"The Tom Sawyer concept," Rick said.

Then with no more stories to tell, he stuck his hands in his pockets, paced the foyer in front of the door, and finally whispered in Uncle Edward's ear loud enough so that I could hear it too, "Isn't it time to go?"

That was all it seemed to take.

Uncle Edward scooped up his keys, flashed a quick glance at the mirror, then turned to me. "Sorry to leave you like this, little Pigeon," he said. "But Rick and I have some business to attend to. I will only be an hour and then we'll go out together."

"It's okay," I said. If I was going to accomplish the task of finding my father, I would need to get started right away. I was there on a mission, and I had only one day and one night to accomplish my goal. Uncle Edward and I were due back home the next morning.

Rick smiled too wide, and shook my hand roughly, as if he were not used to being around children. I saw him even take stock of the apartment, and then move a strobe-like glass globe and the large black figurine of a naked man staring down at his own body to a safe place on top of a bookshelf. It was where I would be sure not to knock them over, although I had not done anything like that in years.

"You can watch TV," Rick offered. "I've got cable. And I believe there's some soda in the refrigerator. And a bathroom over there if you need to freshen up."

I could tell that he was trying to be attentive and polite and I smiled at him. In his dark suit and trim hair he looked somewhat like the mannequins in the department store windows or like the Ken doll Dove used to own; he walked stiffly too, as if he had only recently been brought to life.

"She'll be fine," Uncle Edward said.

He unclipped the barrette on top of my head and smoothed my hair with his fingers before clipping it back. "She's used to being alone."

That was true; in fact right then I was *eager* to be alone.

"It's only one in the afternoon," Uncle Edward continued, although I could see from the clock that it was closer to two. "I'll be back before three, and then we'll go to the museum and afterward we'll have a wonderful dinner. Someplace where we need to dress up nice."

Uncle Edward knelt down before me and put his hands under my chin.

"I want you to be good while we're gone, Pigeon," he said to me, his voice serious. "I don't want you to answer the phone, I don't want you to open the door, and I don't want you to touch anything in this room but the TV."

"Okay," I said. "I won't."

"There are a lot of valuable art pieces here," Rick said. "Make sure she understands that."

"I'm not a baby," I said.

"You're certainly not," Uncle Edward said, kissing me good-bye.

Then he and Rick locked the door behind them, and the neon-bright paintings from the walls, the smooth dark sculptures of nudes, and the jungle-like plants all moved imperceptibly closer to me, eyeing me as if I were an alien landing in their backyard.

I knew I should have begun my search immediately, but for a short while after Uncle Edward left I was just overwhelmed—by the task before me, and even more so by the apartment. It really was only one large room, though, certainly with space for us all. There were ceiling-to-floor windows along one wall, but they were sealed tightly with grey blinds so that only small slats of light escaped into the room. The floor was what looked like grey wood, and all the furniture was muted grey leather, so that it made me feel as if I was not really in the room, but viewing it on a black and white television screen.

The kitchen, I discovered, was not a separate room at all, but only an alcove off the living room. Instead of grey, the kitchen was red and chrome, and all the appliances seemed made not for adults, but for a child, they were so small. When I opened the refrigerator I discovered eight clear plastic bottles of Evian water, one lime, and a round chocolate chip cookie on a napkin with a small precise bite taken out of its side.

Climbing up on a chair, I found that the contents of the cabinets were disappointing as well. Among the china and glassware, the only edible items to be found were five oversize jars of pills and vitamins. Some were small and round, others so large I imagined only a giant could swallow them. And others gave off an odor not unlike dog poop on the bottom of a shoe.

I imagined Rick living entirely off his bottled water and these pills, taking them in place of his morning coffee, juice, a bowl of cereal. Cary had once told me that men who took mass quantities of vitamins were really in search of a woman—did they think the vitamins would help?

"I hate those guys who have names for each of their vitamin pills," Cary had said, and then shrugging at me, he had added, "They're not real men."

This explanation did not seem to make sense, however, and I wondered instead if Rick were very sick, if his doctors had advised him not to eat solid food, but only pills. Then I remembered the cookie and wondered if every so often he cheated, and like a child stole a very small bit of something sweet and good to eat. At any rate, there was no soda, there was no bread or fruit, nor even a small wedge of cheese. There was nothing else.

The only other room in the apartment was a bathroom, but it was unlike any bathroom I had ever seen before. First, there was no door; it was left wide open so that anyone could see you use the toilet or take a bath, brush your teeth. It was also the largest bathroom I had ever seen, with a bright unshaded window up near the ceiling, an exercise bicycle, a rowing machine, and an enormous grey whirlpool still filled with water, though quiet with its mechanisms shut off. I let my hand dangle in the water and felt that it was still warm, as if someone had recently stepped out. There was even a grey towel, still damp, hanging from a rack by the tub.

On the walls were pictures, drawings, photographs, even one large painting, all of people, men and women, using the toilet. Sitting hunched over, wiping their bottoms, naked, dressed, standing up to pee, as if people using the room needed to be reminded what its basic function was for. I suppose in a bathroom like that it was easy to forget.

"One's bathroom habits are not for public viewing and opinion," our mother had once told me when I had forgotten to knock and accidentally walked in on her using the toilet one afternoon. Remembering her words, the flush of my cheeks, I quickly turned away from the pictures, embarrassed as if I had walked in on them as well, although of course they were not real people. I splashed my face with some cool water from the tap, and then dried the sink and the faucet with the towel from the rack, making sure I left it all as I had found it.

When I re-entered the main room everything was still. I thought about my father's postcard, wondering if there had been any clues as to where he was in New York City. I did not know where to begin; when my mother wanted to find someone, she looked in the phone book, but I did not think this would help me in my search. I needed a better plan, one that took thought and preparation.

I sat back down on the couch, the leather making that strange funny sound as I did so—scrunch scrunch—as I shifted my body to try to get comfortable. Leaning back, I pulled up my pant leg, and counted my mosquito bites. The mosquitoes had been nasty that summer, particularly in the late afternoon when I often played in the sand where they huddled in buzzing pockets low in the air. Examining my skin, I discovered I had four on one ankle alone and I scratched one until it bled, then stopped the trickle with my finger.

"Scratching anything that itches causes scars for life," our mother had taught us all when we were very young.

I believed her, and knew I would one day as an adult stare down at a small, almost imperceptible, scar on my ankle and remember that day in New York.

Then, in a burst of energy and renewed courage, I rose from the couch and set out to look for our father. I could go to our old apartment—it was in New York, and I was in New York—and I would find our father there. That was the kind of logic I had back then when I was young; a logic that I believe now protects us from too much hurt and that we lose as we grow older.

THE LOCKS on Rick's door caused me no problem, and in the elevator I was easily able to reach the lowest button marked with a capital G. A woman with two fawn-colored Great Danes let me go before her, and the doorman smiled at me and tipped his blue hat.

Once I was outside, the heat of the city nearly flattened me with its intensity, and the traffic in the street seemed particularly loud and daunting only because I had been at the beach for so many months, and had already forgotten what that many people and cars on narrow streets sounded like. I had never traveled alone in New York City before and did not know that the streets lay in grids, that at each intersection there were two names.

I did not even completely remember my old address. It was either 98 West something, or something West 98th. I thought I would just come across the street if I walked far enough; I certainly knew what it looked like, the row of grey buildings on either side, the front steps with their iron railings, the small evenly spaced trees with their sad scattering of leaves, their wire fencing protecting them from dogs and who knows what else.

At age five, I did not realize the impossibility of my task—to find an apartment in New York City with no address, to find among all of the people, only my father.

Nonetheless I started out walking up the avenue towards a row of buildings that, although unlike my old apartment, were closer to it than the one I had just left. I saw men returning to their offices from lunch with their suit jackets slung over their shoulders, and one woman, dressed otherwise impeccably in a crisp blue-and-white dress, walking barefoot down the street, carrying her high heels and nylons in her hands.

Another woman held onto the arms of her two young children, a boy and a girl, and she kept tugging at them as if they were recalcitrant wagons with a wheel missing or a bent axle. I smiled at them, but they did not seem to catch my eye.

I had only walked three blocks when, already tired, I spotted the recognizable large white sign of the pharmacy, its frosted glass windows filled with promotions for weight-loss programs and discounted syringes. The store was immediately familiar as if I had been there before or had been dreaming about it for many nights now. I knew. It was the pharmacy where our father worked.

I entered it at the same time as a very large woman whose flowered dress clung too tightly to her in the heat.

"You go ahead, little girl," she said to me as she held the door open, and I squeezed past the small remaining space she left in the doorway, smelling her odor and dampness as I did so.

Once inside, the woman breathed an enormous sigh, and smiled, showing all her teeth. "Air-conditioning," she said to me. "It's a little bit of heaven. Don't you think so?"

She asked as if she really expected me to answer, as if she waited upon my response, and I nodded my head vigorously in agreement.

"A woman of my size was not made for heat," she went on. With a small deprecating laugh, she walked over to the cosmetics aisle along the side wall, glancing back for only a moment to see if perhaps I might have followed, only to find me still standing alone.

There were perhaps twenty aisles in the store altogether, all filled with a collection of items deemed necessary for daily life. In addition to the cosmetics there was an aisle with nothing but cold remedies, and another with baby products—diapers and powders, lotions, bottles, small cans of formula. There were products for the teeth and for the bath, racks containing sunglasses and another with glasses that magnified words for those who had difficulty reading, and three shelves devoted to hair care, and another two filled strictly with suntan lotions. There was even my favorite aisle, the one filled with toys—coloring books and crayons, cheap plastic trucks and cars, jigsaw puzzles, and an odd assortment of board games. Yet however interesting any of these individual items might have been, none of them was what I was looking for.

"Where do you keep the drugs," I asked the young man at the checkout counter who couldn't have been much older than Dove, and he grunted. He was fiddling with the machine that produced the lottery tickets—it seemed as if a button was broken or stuck.

"You mean the prescriptions?" he asked, without looking down.

"Yes," I nodded. "That's what I want."

He seemed to fix the machine then, or simply abandon it for later, and finally looked at me. "Aren't you a bit young for drugs?" he said, smirking. "Don't you mean you want the candy?"

"You heard what the girl said." It was the large woman in the flowered dress; she was standing behind me now, her hands filled with her purchases—pink-colored liquids and compacts.

"The prescription drugs are kept in the back of the store," she said to me, and not being able to point with her hands so occupied, she shifted her entire body in that direction instead.

"Yea, that's where they are," the checkout clerk said.

"Do you want me to bring you there?" I heard the woman ask me kindly, but I was already on my way.

In the back was a sign reading Rx, and the high white counter our father stood behind. I had watched him at work before; he had every so often brought Dove, Robin, and me with him on a slow summer morning to this very store. We had played cards in the back and drunk colas out of the can, and I had watched him perform his duties—mixing up strange colored liquids, weighing pills on a silver scale, recording doctors' ID numbers in a small black book.

A man with a green ponytail now stood leaning against the counter, waiting for a prescription to be filled; his eyes were closed and he was humming to himself. I wondered if he had some disease that had turned his hair green, if that were his illness. I wondered if there was a medicine that could help a condition like that. There was a very pretty woman waiting there too, coolly checking out her nails, which were long and painted a bright shiny red. But on the back of her left hand was an uncovered sore, large and wet with pus—it seemed that no one in the pharmacy was free from imperfections.

Then I saw him. There behind the white counter where he always was. His back was to me, but I could see his dark hair, large shoulders, a white lab coat. He was mixing up a prescription, slowly pouring yellow pills from one large bottle into a small plastic vial, and I knew from the way he moved his shoulders, to the shape and size of his head, that it was him. Still, I walked up closer just to be sure. I knew that coat. I had smelled it. I had even fallen asleep on it. It was our father.

"Daddy," I called, and jumped up as if I might reach him, touch him. "It's me, Pigeon. I came to find you."

And when he didn't at first turn around, I said it again, louder, "Daddy!" So that everyone in the store could have heard me.

The green-haired ponytail man opened his eyes, stopped humming, and two other men turned around as if they were each expecting young daughters of their own. Even the woman stopped looking at her nails for a moment and covered her sore with the opposite hand.

"Daddy!" I was shouting it now. And then my father, from behind the white counter, did turn around, peered down at me.

"Can I help you, miss," he asked in a voice so unlike my father's voice it hurt my ears even to listen, and I realized at once my obvious and horrible mistake.

It was an older man's face that looked down at me, not at all familiar, with a large fleshy nose and reddened eyes—strange and frightening.

"Yes, what would you like?" the pharmacist said.

"You're not my daddy," I said.

"Well, of course not," he said, and when he laughed I felt my face grow hot, my ears pound.

Soon they were all laughing. And although they could not have really known, I believed they were laughing at me—at my mistake, my embarrassment, at my foolishness at thinking my father would still be there. It could not have lasted long—only a moment—but I would always remember it, as a teenager, and as an adult. And I would remember that pharmacist's face, like the kind that haunts you in nightmares. It does haunt me. I see it sometimes instead of my real father's face in the glass of a shop window on the street, or in the faces of men I have known and even loved, and on hot summer nights when I am preparing myself for bed.

"Oh dear, the little girl is lost," I heard a woman say.

It was the fat one again from the cosmetics aisle, and I saw her shuffle in her slow gait towards me. "I'll help you. I'll help you," she said.

But I could not possibly have waited for her assistance. Without more than a backward glance, I was off running through the aisle of candy and cigars and men's razors, and out through the front glass door until I felt once again the heat of the sun on my head, the smell of a New York summer.

I ran back the three blocks to Rick's apartment and the doorman let me in and directed me in the right direction, back up the elevator and down the long hall. But the door was locked and I did not have the keys to get back inside. I rang the bell, I knocked, and when no one answered, and with no other alternative, I sat down on the carpeted floor in the hallway, my back against the wall, and waited for Uncle Edward's return.

Often when we are left alone waiting for long periods of time our minds begin to see things our eyes, with their far more limited scope and range, can not. I remember Dove once telling me that while waiting for anything, anyone, she could suddenly understand her entire algebra lesson, remember complete pages out of her history text, recite lines of poetry that had previously eluded her. But

Dove, who had never been a particularly skillful student, also said that once she was through waiting she forgot all that had just a moment ago seemed so clear. She often wondered if the brighter students were only those girls who were perpetually waiting—for their breasts to grow, for their faces to clear up, for a boy to call, for a first kiss.

Having not started school at the time, I had my own theory. Perhaps it was the discomfort of waiting that did it. The dreadful building-up of minutes, hours, time, until all your senses seemed to disappear and what was left was you sitting there on the floor in a strange apartment building, your head hot with impatience. Until that too was gone, and only your mind was there with hardly a body or head attached.

That was how it was for me, and I began thinking about things I had long forgotten, although not in any particular sequence. I remembered our mother surreptitiously giving me a chocolate heart the previous Valentine's Day, saying nothing. And I saw Dove and Robin and our mother all playing ring-around-the-rosie with me right after I learned how to walk, only I kept falling down too early until we all stopped singing and only danced and fell, danced and fell. There was the bedroom I used to share with Robin, and I saw Dove sneaking in late at night so that we could all whisper together under the low glow of her flashlight. A morning we had eaten pancakes with raspberries so sweet we had all agreed together to eat them and nothing else for as long as we lived.

Remembering all this, I thought my life had been okay. And I thought of a hot day in New York (it must have been the summer before); our father dressed in a white long-sleeved shirt, the sleeves rolled up, baring his pale arms. Our mother's hair was pulled back in a ponytail and she was wearing one of our father's white tee shirts and what looked like blue-striped boxer shorts, although they certainly weren't stylish for women back then.

We had no air-conditioning, only fans, and our parents sat in front of the open window hoping for some cool air on that hot humid day. Our father was doing the crossword puzzle, mother was watching him do it, and I was watching them both. Listened to the scratch of our father's pen as he filled in a word, heard the soft murmuring of mother's voice as she supplied an answer for him. For the most part, however, they were quite still. Until at one point I saw our father lift up mother's ponytail with his hand and, pursing his lips together, blow softly along the nape of her neck.

"Oh, that feels so good," mother said. "So suddenly cool."

Our father laughed, and upon seeing me, they called me over so that I could feel it too, the breeze that was our father's breath, so that small bumps raised on my arms.

Our apartment was close and dark as it always was, filled with furniture that had belonged to someone long since dead. The table-tops were void of knickknacks, vases, bowls, the walls were empty of pictures, coverings of any kind. Robin must have been in the bedroom that summer morning, Dove out with friends. There was nothing much to remember at all, just our father, mother, me all sharing the large blue chair by the window.

Our father put his crossword puzzle down. "If I am good for nothing else," he said to mother and me then, "let me be known for cooling off two beautiful girls."

His voice was as clear and as real as if he were still with me, sitting beside me on the hall carpeting, pursing his lips, blowing his breath across the back of my neck.

But it was Uncle Edward who eventually came to sit beside me. He strode out of the elevator, and when he saw me on the floor, his mouth opened wide as if he were about to scream.

"What are you doing here?" he said with alarm in his voice. "I said for you to wait inside."

Then I told him what I had done—told him about my plan to find my father, told him about leaving the apartment, and finding the pharmacy where I was sure my father worked. I told him the entire story.

"I was sure it was him," I said. "I was so sure."

"Little Pigeon," he said, and his voice was no longer angry, but quiet and sad. "How do you think you could have found your father?"

He sat down next to me outside the apartment door. Our shoulders touched; he didn't seem to mind that his suit was getting dirty and wrinkled from the carpet.

"New York is a big city," he said. "There are thousands of pharmacies and they all look alike. And millions of apartment buildings, and millions and millions of people. I'm sorry."

I knew what he was telling me was true, had perhaps known it in some strange way even before we had left that morning. Although

I don't believe I had ever felt so unbearably sad, strangely I did not cry.

"You mean I'm not going to find my father?" I said.

"I guess that's what I'm saying," Uncle Edward said, and he shrugged.

"I was never going to find him," I said. It was not a question.

"I guess not," Uncle Edward said.

"Then why did you invite me to come to New York?" I said.

"I just didn't want you to be so unhappy. I wanted you to have a little fun."

"What's so fun about this?" I said.

Uncle Edward sighed. "I'm sorry. I didn't think it all the way through."

That made sense to me, not thinking things through. In fact I had been accused of doing just that myself. "It's okay," I said. I put my hand next to his larger hand and he placed it in the warmth of his palm.

"I suppose you'll have to wait for him to come back on his own," Uncle Edward said.

"I suppose so."

Our backs were both against the wall, our legs stretched out before us—Uncle Edward's long legs with his big black shoes, my short ones with my Keds—and we stared straight ahead in the dimly lit hall. We were quiet, each thinking his or her own thoughts.

Finally, Uncle Edward spoke. "This isn't going to be your last disappointment, Little Pigeon," he said. "It doesn't get easier."

"I know that," I said.

"But there's always a reason," Uncle Edward went on. "At least that's what I've always been told," and it seemed as if he had ceased speaking to me and was instead only saying aloud what he had been thinking inside. "There are reasons men disappear and children are left alone. There's a reason why you didn't find him."

Then, as if it had just occurred to him, he added, "If you had actually found your father and he were to discover that Dove was pregnant it would kill him. Just kill him."

"Dove was always his favorite," I said.

Uncle Edward looked at me, shook his head. "You're something else," he said.

"You bet I am."

We never made it to the museum, but we dressed up that night, Uncle Edward and I—he in a tuxedo and bow tie, I in my one fancy dress, an old hand-me-down from Dove—and we took a carriage ride through Central Park. The night sky was filled with stars, the moon was a silvery bright crescent, the park was whispery with strollers walking arm in arm, and the driver and the horse both wore matching straw hats with live daisies slipped into the blue silk bands. Uncle Edward had bought our dinner at a small gourmet shop near Rick's apartment, and we ate it now—chicken salad with grapes, orange and black pasta, hearts of palm—out of Styrofoam containers, being careful not to spill any when the carriage stopped short or hit a rut in the road.

It was a lovely ride even with all expectations of finding my father gone. Uncle Edward spoke to me of grown-up matters I barely understood—art galleries, co-op prices, a shipping firm he knew something about. And he spoke even for a short while of our mother and himself.

We were on dessert—Uncle Edward had produced out of his shopping bag two fruit tarts, which we now ate messily between us.

"Having a father isn't everything," Uncle Edward told me, as we each licked our fingers clean. "Ours used to watch our every move. Told us what to wear, what to say, what to do, and smacked us around if we didn't obey. Even your mother."

"He sounds mean," I said.

"He was," Uncle Edward said. "And when your mother and I were little we always dreamed of running away from him. To New York, in fact. And we imagined we would take a carriage ride just like this one."

"Did you ever do it," I asked.

"We never even came close," said Uncle Edward. "We were frightened and never did anything but whine about how terrible we had it. We were both simply awful."

It was not said with particular sorrow nor humor, but I think instead with a certain growing acceptance of whom they had been, what they were today.

"I don't think you're awful," I said. I could see the carriage was fast approaching the circle we had left from—the lights from the cars, the stores, the big hotels, the fountain quickly surrounded us in a sea of noise—and I knew we would go back to Rick's apartment where I would be put to bed in that strange room and ignored.

"I really don't," I said.

"You don't know me very well, little Pigeon," Uncle Edward said. "And that is fortunate for both of us."

But when the carriage stopped, and he reached over to hand the driver his fare and tip, he kissed me on the head and said, "Thank you though, just the same."

EVERYONE HAD heard of my failure in New York even before I reached home the next day, and they were unusually sympathetic. Out on the back porch, Dove braided my hair for me and let me wear a bracelet that Stan had given to her at the beginning of the summer, before their troubles with the baby.

"I won't be needing it anymore," Dove said as she pushed the small clasp closed around my wrist.

I extended my arm and we both admired the bracelet for a moment—the glint of the gold links in the sun, the small sapphire in the center.

"It really is beautiful," Dove said. "Isn't it."

"It really is," I said.

Still later in the early evening before dinner, both Robin and Cary came unannounced into my room where I was on the floor playing with my paper dolls. They did not sit down with me, but admired my work just the same. Robin assured me that I couldn't have possibly found our father—no one could.

"Did Edith tell you that?" I asked him. "Did she read it in the cards?"

"No," he admitted with a shrug, and a small embarrassed smile. "It's just something I figured out on my own. You know I'm getting quite good at reading the future myself."

"You should have warned me before I went," I told him.

"Yes, you should have," Cary said.

"I didn't know what you were going to do," Robin said, and then incongruously, "I think I hoped you might actually find him. I think we all did."

"Not me," Cary said. "I hope the guy is gone for good. Lost in space. I'm glad you didn't find him."

He twirled his hands around my head and when he opened them they were filled with a chocolate bar each.

"For you," Cary said and he let them drop to the floor. "For doing such a super job."

It was our mother who surprisingly was the kindest of all. After dinner she ordered Cary and Robin to clean up, and she led me to her room and closed the door behind us.

We sat down on the bed, the old soft mattress curving under our small weight, and mother traced the thread of the bedspread with her finger, over and over again in circles. I looked at the blank walls, at our mother's Power of Power cap on her dresser, at my own bare knees.

"I'm sorry you didn't find your father," she finally said.

"I thought I could do it," I said. "I thought I would just get to New York and he would be there."

"You did your best," mother said. When she looked at me I could see that her eyes were red and moist as if she were about to cry.

"You told me that Brother Tank taught us that if we wanted something badly enough we should just go out and take it."

"Did I say that?" mother said.

I nodded.

Our mother then rubbed her cheeks in a rhythmic motion; they were smooth and freckled from the sun. She seemed to be considering what I had said. Her response, however, had nothing to do with Brother Tank or finding our father.

"You've grown up pretty quickly," she said to me. "You're much older than I was at your age."

I wasn't sure how that could be, how if you were both the same age, one could be older, but I said nothing.

"And you've been a really good girl," mother went on. She didn't look at me when she said this, but instead rose from the bed, and I could feel it shift after she was gone, the way I imagined a house must when it is empty, after its inhabitants have left. She walked over to her dresser, examined her face in the mirror.

"I've tried to be a good mother," she said not to me now, but to her reflection. "Don't you think I have? Don't you think so?"

We were both embarrassed then; we said nothing for a while. I wriggled on the bed, chewed my lip. Our mother fiddled with her orange cap, turning its visor upward and down.

Then something magical happened, at least in my mind it was magical. Or at the very least unexpected and rare. Mother walked back over to the bed and from underneath it she reached and pulled out a small yellow box that I recognized at once as being from the local clothing store.

"This is for you," she said, handing it to me.

And when I opened it quickly, holding my breath, I discovered inside a beautiful new swimsuit. Not one handed down from Dove, nor bought for a dollar at a used clothing store, but a new one with its tags still attached, selected with only me in mind. It was the purple one they had featured in the window—stretchy and brightly flowered, with a bow in the back, and just my size.

"I love it," I said. "It's perfect." And it was.

"Remember, Pigeon," mother said. "Material possessions do not define who we are."

"I know that," I said.

But she ran her hand across the smooth silky fabric of the suit. She was smiling at me.

"Well, don't just sit there," she said finally. "Let's see how it looks."

Giddy with love, I hurried to my room eager to try the new bathing suit on. And anxious, as well, as if this wonderful fleeting moment could somehow be mine to keep or, through further mishandling and folly, to lose.

Learning the Truth

Sometime during the first week of August, Edith displayed a new sign in front of her fortune-telling shop. Now, instead of there being just the one worn sign reading 'Fortunes Told, Fortunes Read, $20/each, Other Services Available,' there was a new sign below it. This one was larger and there was a black and white photograph tacked onto its side. The new sign read: FEATURING ROBIN, THE "BOY WONDER." HE KNOWS ALL, and the photograph was a still of Batman and Robin, who were popular from the prime time television show; they were dressed in their crime-fighting gear, their masked faces serious, earnest, ready for action. But it was our Robin who would be telling the fortunes, our Robin who had gotten himself a new full-time job.

We all saw the sign, of course; you couldn't miss it if you walked up the boardwalk, even if you were not accustomed to looking at Edith's dilapidated shop. The sign was that large, and that freshly painted, and the words HE KNOWS ALL were in a fluorescent shade of pink.

"Ha!" Dove said when she saw it for the first time. I noticed her hands splayed across her stomach right where the baby lay waiting to be born. But there was only the slightest sign that there was a baby there at all.

"So the kid's smart," Dove said. "That doesn't mean he knows everything."

"It's hard to believe he would even get taken in by something like this," said Uncle Edward. "What a shame."

"Robin, the boy wonder," I marveled.

It was our mother, however, who was the first one to know about the sign. She came home from work one evening escorted by Cary, but instead of the two of them retiring into the living room alone, she hurried in before him, the belt buckle of her dress askew, her upper body bent forward as if she could not enter the room quickly enough. When she reached the bottom of the stairs in the foyer she shouted up in an angry voice for Robin to come, now, and quickly we both obeyed.

He and I had already been watching from the top window in my room—had heard the car pull in—and at the sound of her voice, Robin padded barefoot down the stairs while I followed a short distance behind.

In stockinged feet, she stood there, her black flat-heeled shoes in her hands and she tapped one quickly, impatiently against the banister as she waited. Behind her, in the open doorway, Cary leaned, with his tie loosened, sleeves rolled up, a smug look on his face. We were not his children, his problem. Yet I could see from the look on our mother's face, hear from the tone of her voice, and Robin could too, that this news was not pleasant for her.

"Robin," she began, her voice as taut as the blue veins that pulsed in her neck. "Do you know what I found out today?"

Of course he did, but perhaps wisely said nothing. Together, like two mute children, we stood there on the steps dressed in our light summer pajamas. Mine were sprinkled with yellow flowers, Robin's striped like a baseball uniform, and his arm, which he had draped over the banister, was like a thin curled branch, his legs two long sticks. The slightest touch might have sent him tumbling forward, yet he did not appear frightened as I was, three steps above him.

I picked at the skin on my arms which had long since burned in the sun and was now peeling in strips I rolled between my fingers, as I looked anxiously from Robin to our mother and then back to Robin again, waiting for something terrible to occur.

"Do you know what happened at work today?" mother rhetorically asked again. Cary, who presumably already knew, grunted in the background. "Do you know who came by?"

It turned out, according to our mother, that just that afternoon Edith had visited the movie theater where mother worked. She had come asking for any photographs or posters of Batman and Robin that the theater might own, and she was even willing to pay the current price.

"I told her we only carried film memorabilia, not promotions for television cartoon characters," mother said.

"It's not a cartoon," I piped in. "Batman and Robin are real people."

"Nevertheless," mother said. "I told her to look elsewhere. Then, in that simply awful way she told me what the sign was for."

Mother gave a tortured look at Robin and although I could only see the side of his face it seemed, however unlikely, as if he were smiling. One of those spontaneous smiles that starts out of nowhere, and feels like a giggle.

"Wipe that off your face," mother said. It looked as if she were going to do it for him, her shoe held posed right up close to his mouth.

With aplomb, Robin dared her. "Go right ahead."

But instead, she caught her breath, continued. "Edith told me my son was working for her now. She said he reads the future through the cards."

"I can," Robin said, standing up straighter, holding his slim shoulders erect. If one can look confident wearing short-sleeved baseball pajamas, then Robin did.

And I realized that somewhere along the way my brother had stopped asking so many questions—they had seemed endless at one point—and was now providing us with the answers.

"I'm a fortune-teller," he told her.

"No," mother said. "No, you're not."

But you could see her realizing it was no longer within her command. By now she was dropping her shoes to the floor with a clunk, and she leaned forward to cup her hand around Robin's neck.

"No one can predict the future," she insisted. "It is out of our hands."

"What about Ouiji boards?" I asked, still from a safe distance up the stairs. Dove used to own one and we had sat on the floor of our old apartment facing each other with our fingertips lightly on the pointer, waiting for it to tell Dove who her next boyfriend might be, whom she would marry, how many children she could expect, and whether I would be allowed to stay up an extra half hour past my bed time. Sadly, the board had not made the move with us to Uncle Edward's.

"Ouiji boards are toys," Robin said in a strained voice.

"Yes," mother agreed.

Finally, she had released her grip on him, tucked her offending hand within her own armpit. Looking closely, I could see the four red marks her fingers had left at the nape of Robin's neck.

"And so are tarot cards," she said. "Our lives are not predetermined, we make our own futures."

"I can so read the future," Robin still maintained. "I get paid for doing it too."

And Cary, who had been quiet during all this, finally spoke up from the doorway, his low deep voice sounding alien after our mother's hysteria. "How much is the crazy broad paying you?" he asked. "What are you taking in?"

"Stay out of this. It doesn't concern you," mother snapped at him.

Robin ignored her. "I get twenty percent of every client I bring in," he said. "But the money is beside the point."

"What is the point?" mother asked.

"I have the gift," Robin said.

"The gift?" She was shrieking now, her voice curling up my neck like a gust of cold wind so that I involuntarily shivered.

"I heard Edith say that," I whispered. "She said he was blessed."

"Blessed!" mother screamed.

Cary chuckled. "That old crook is going to take him for all that he's worth. Or more."

With that, our mother had had enough. She bent over, picked up one of her shoes, and flung it at Cary so that it flew upward in a fast spiral. It missed him, however, ricocheting against the wall above him and leaving a black smudge on the pristine walls of Uncle Edward's house.

I had never seen mother so angry with Cary, had never seen that particular look directed at him. In fact, in the last few weeks they had been closer than ever. She had even been calling him her "Eagle," and threatened sometimes to fly away with him. As if she could fly, I had thought when I heard the pet name; but I had been nervous about her departure all the same.

"Imagine it, Pigeon," she had said to me, and I had grown terrified doing just that, imagining her disappearing from our lives.

But not now. I could have wished her gone, her face red with rage at all in her life that was so completely out of her control.

Stepping back, Cary cocked his head to look at the spot on the wall, broke out into a wide foolish grin. "Lousy aim, Joan," he said, "but what a sweet-looking arm."

He roared then with laughter, and Robin, whether through sheer nervousness, or more likely that by standing up to our mother he had momentarily entered into the league of men, joined in.

It was not a passing fancy, however. Robin took his new job and gift most seriously. Seven days a week, he was out of the house by nine in the morning and usually didn't arrive back home until nine at night. I missed having him home on the weekends, and for lunch and dinner, but he told me that Edith needed him, and besides he preferred to eat on the job.

He also began making predictions. He predicted that our mother would slip on spilled soda at the movie theater and twist her ankle; and that she would be given a promotion by Brother Tank—she would sit on the stage with him, bring him cool water when his throat was parched, wipe his brow when he perspired. And both came to pass.

He predicted that Cary would get in an accident in his Mustang; and the very next morning, while Cary pulled into a parking space at the casino where he worked, a fellow employee nicked his fender. "Some old coot who should have had his license taken away years ago," Cary said.

Robin also predicted that the Phillies would lose the next four games, that there would be three days of sunshine when the weather report had called for rain, and that I would find a Kennedy dollar coin in the sand—and all these predictions came true.

"Edith says I'm a treasure," Robin told us.

"Mere coincidences," mother said.

"A treasure," said Cary. "I'll just bet you are."

Robin even revealed to me that Dove would get married by the end of the summer and that our father would be at the wedding.

"What do you think of that," he said to me, his face bright with the news.

"I knew he would come back," I said.

Even with my failure in New York, it was still easy enough for me to believe that our father would be there to watch his eldest and favorite daughter get married.

But married to whom? Stan had not been around in weeks, and we were not even to mention his name. There were no other young men coming to call. Instead, it was Joe Winter who had taken to picking up Dove for work and driving her back home again late at night. We lived only a few blocks from the restaurant—she could easily walk—but Joe Winter had learned of her pregnancy and he seemed to have taken her condition to heart.

"A girl with a bun in the oven," I heard him say, "shouldn't walk anywhere in this heat."

"Never mind the fact that she's on her feet the entire shift at his place," Cary said under his breath.

It was clear that Cary had never liked Joe Winter. "The kind of man that would leave his best friend to die in the dirt," Cary always said of him. He cautioned Dove that spending any more time with a man like Joe Winter might make people wonder who the father of her child really was.

"The kind of man who would deny the child was his," mother added.

"I don't like him either," I said.

Of course we all knew Uncle Edward liked him. They had been friends for years and still went out together on the occasional odd evening when Edward was in town. But Dove, for some strange reason, liked him as well. He wasn't bad-looking with his thick dark hair, large white teeth, but Dove had never fallen for conventional good looks. Perhaps it was the sky blue convertible Cadillac he drove. Or the way he took her arm in his and escorted her down our walk as if she were someone famous, or at the very least someone dear and special, in need of assistance. Or more likely Dove was just lonely being pregnant, with Stan in New York, and all the other girls her age in their bikinis playing volleyball on the beach and kissing their boyfriends until their lips looked red and smudged.

I suppose she must have had some regrets with Stan no longer visiting or calling. For a while I know he had tried to convince her to marry him. He would call her once or twice a day and I could hear her exasperated voice over the phone.

"I'm just seventeen for God's sake," I had heard her tell him. "I can't settle down yet."

But she must have known that a baby would settle her down for good.

Recently, however, Stan had stopped calling, and now here was Joe Winter to take his place.

I do not know for a fact whatever happened between them. Of

course, there was the message on the side of the restaurant—JOE LOVES DOVE—but Joe had had that promptly whitewashed over and soon it became old news that few talked about anymore.

"Just some stupid prankster," Joe Winter had said of the message as the workers rolled their white paint over the side of his building. Or more likely some jealous waitress, for Dove did get all the best shifts, and she certainly made far more than the other waitresses in tips.

But there *was* something Dove and Joe shared between them. It wasn't just that he drove her to work and back, although that might have been enough. It was the way they looked after each other when one's back was turned or walking away—a furtive suspicious look that jealous lovers sometimes have. And it was the way they carelessly touched, not just in the obvious places, but behind the ear, the space above the lip, a curved elbow. Private, intimate places.

He also teased my sister relentlessly, telling her there was nothing so sexy as a pregnant woman. Around her he could barely control himself, and although Dove always said "Oh, please," or "You do go on," perhaps it wasn't really teasing at all.

Although I disliked Joe, I could understand my sister's need. I, too, was particularly lonely that month of August. It wasn't until I was older that I learned that young children customarily had babysitters when their mothers were out, someone mature to watch over them. But allowing a stranger into our house would never have occurred to our mother. I was always left alone, always had been. And with all hope of finding our father gone, now I could only wait for him to return on his own.

Since our trip to New York, Uncle Edward was away even more often, and when he was home it seemed as if he avoided me. As if he were embarrassed by my lack of success or perhaps by something else he could not name.

Due to the heat, the air-conditioned theater where our mother worked was busier than ever—they had added two additional shows a day, one very early in the morning and one late at night—and mother alternated working each one. Due to that, we saw less of Cary as well, although he still came by every Thursday night with our dinner (now it was usually only Dove and I who ate) before going to see Brother Tank.

More popular than ever, Brother Tank had made the front page of not only the local paper, but the *Philadelphia Inquirer* as well, which only very occasionally covered the news in our small beach community. He was alternately being hailed both as a prophet and an entrepreneur, and our mother told us that his new followers who came to see him did not seem nearly as devoted nor as sincere as the ones from the past.

"They only come to gawk," Mother said.

"Still they bring in the cash," said Cary.

"I hate to think it has come to that," mother said. "I always thought there was a lot more to it than money."

"You're an easy mark," Cary said.

But they continued to attend his meetings in Atlantic City. Cary, perhaps, just for our mother's company alone, our mother because she still did believe, still worked for him as well. And every now and then she could be heard reiterating something he had said— "We are solid, not water that can fit in anyone's jar," and "Bite the day!" There was a copy of his commandments tacked up in every room of the house. They contained little solace for me.

EACH NIGHT, I was pulled out of sleep by the sound of Joe Winter's long Cadillac screeching fast around the corner and Dove's laugh like a solo bird twittering in the night. Joe liked to listen to Bette Midler, one song in particular—her version of "Do You Want to Dance"—which he played over and over on his tape deck, full volume, with the Cadillac's top down. I would awaken to this music and already be at the window when the car pulled up to the curb in front of the house. I would watch as they sat there close together in the dark car listening to the song just once more, swaying their heads moodily back and forth, as if they were dancing, alone, just the two of them.

"Do you want to dance under the moonlight. Hug me, kiss me, all through the night. Oh, baby, do you want to dance?"

The words were not sad, but it always seemed a melancholy song to me, particularly the way Bette Midler phrased it, and I pictured a woman pleading to a man, with clutched hands, to dance with her, touch her, love her, when he really never would.

I was surprised that Dove would listen to the song so often—she had always been much more of a rock and roll fan—but not only did she listen to it in Joe Winter's car; I also often heard her singing snatches of the song throughout the day in her small sweet voice, moving to some inner rhythm and beat. It seemed as if she had made the song her own, and when she sang it, it was saddest of all.

Just when I thought I understood the tempo of our lives—the times when the members of my family were home, then out, then home again, whole weeks going by in an orderly fashion—something would disrupt the routine. Whether it was Uncle Edward suddenly blowing in through the door from one of his trips, or Cary surprising me at lunchtime with a handful of chips from the casino for me to count, or mother waking me up one morning before the sun had risen just because she said she hadn't seen my face in some time—disruptions were always imminent. And just when I thought I understood Dove and Joe Winter, I found I no longer did.

Although Dove was not wearing maternity clothes yet, you could see the change in her. A slight paling of her face, a roundness below the chin, her clothes fitting snugger. She took to wearing one-piece suits on the beach instead of a bikini. And I caught her crying in front of the mirror one day before work.

She had not yet put on her makeup, nor even brushed her hair, and was dressed only in her underpants and bra. They were both made of white lace with a small pink budded flower pressed between her breasts, and I could see just the slightest of swells above the elastic of her panties. There was a defined band of white where her bathing suit straps had crossed her shoulders and back, so pure it made you want to rest your finger atop the skin, to protect her if only in some insubstantial way.

"I'm so ugly," she said to her reflection. "So fat."

Of course she was neither ugly nor fat, but still beautiful; but I do not think she would have believed me if I had told her so.

"My life will never be the same," she continued. She had spotted me finally, and was speaking more to me now than to the mirror. "I'll never go anywhere, do anything. I'll carry this baby inside me forever."

"Only a bit more than four months," I said.

"That's forever," she said. Spreading her fingers out, she pressed them against her stomach. "I can feel the baby moving now," she told me. "It kicks and thrashes its arms, just to annoy me."

"You can feel it move?" I said.

I was astonished; I had not known that a baby could actually move within the taut confines of my sister's stomach.

"Do you want to feel it?" she asked me, and when I nodded and approached her, she took my hands in her own and placed them on the small rise of her belly.

"I don't feel anything," I said, and then suddenly I did. It was a small spasm, like a flip-flop beneath the surface of her skin. I bit my lip to stop myself from smiling.

"That's what I suffer through," Dove said. "Now do you see?"

I am sure to many my sister may have seemed selfish, complaining about something she had not only wanted, but had fought our mother and Uncle Edward to keep. But that would be because they did not understand her—that she approached all new and frightening things like a cat with its fur sticking up along its spine.

Dove's face without makeup, however, was blameless, smooth like an infant's, with just a splash of freckles across her nose. They were new since her pregnancy. Her hair was such a lovely light shade of red, so thick and long that you only wanted to sink your face in it for a moment and all your troubles would disappear. I loved Dove when I looked at her; and even today when I see photographs of her from that time I know why—her often sharp voice, her shortcomings are not apparent in her young face, and there is an inner strength in her eyes and the thrust of her jaw that made her more attractive still.

Crying again, Dove pressed her hands together as if in prayer.

"What would I do without you, Pigeon?" she said to me. "You're the only one who listens."

Then, with utter resignation, I learned the real reason for her tears; Joe Winter was laying her off.

"He doesn't think I should work any longer," Dove revealed. "He doesn't think an unmarried pregnant girl will do much for his business."

"He can't fire you," I said. "He's crazy about you."

"Perhaps," Dove said doubtfully. "But look at me." She was still crying as she touched the small rise of her stomach. "I'm such an incredible fool," she said.

"No, you're not," I protested. "Everyone loves you."

But Dove did not really need my encouragement. She had already gotten a hold of herself, and with one last choking sob, she lifted her head and began to vigorously wipe her face with a tissue. With a steady hand, she applied her lipstick, flicked a brush of pink blush across each cheek, pulled her hair back, twisted it, and fastened it at the nape of her neck. Rising, she picked up her white uniform from where it lay across the back of her chair and slipped it neatly over her head, smoothed it at her waist and in the front.

"I've got two weeks to turn in this hideous thing and pick up my last check," she said without looking at me. "Then I'm through with the only job I ever had."

"You never wanted to be a waitress anyway," I reminded her.

"You're right," she said. "I don't know why I'm so damn sappy these days. Just give me a slap when I get like this."

As if to demonstrate her point, she slapped her own cheeks a couple of times, then took my hand and pressed it curled against her lips so that they left a smudge of red right below my knuckles. I did not wash that hand all afternoon, not even before bed, when I placed it against my own face and smelled her perfume, like raspberries, in the dark of our room.

That night I dreamed about my birthday. It was in September and the beach was deserted again. Our mother had decorated the back porch with balloons and streamers, and there was a large cake in the center of the table with lit candles that kept blowing out in the swift breeze. Only the cake did not really look like a birthday cake, but was white and tiered as if for someone's wedding, and there was a figurine of the groom and bride sitting on the very top.

"Happy Birthday," mother said in the dream. Cary gave my cheeks a pinch.

But before I had a chance to open their gifts, I looked out onto the beach and saw walking toward us through the sand our father. He looked the same as I remembered, only dressed not in his white pharmacist jacket, but in a black tuxedo, crisp white shirt, patent leather shoes. There was a small yellow rose in his lapel.

Standing beside him, holding onto his arm, was Dove. She wore a lace wedding gown that pulled across and accentuated her pregnant stomach, much bigger in my dream, and on her head lay a wreath of pastel flowers. Her red hair blew across her face and like a mane in the back as the wind picked up from the ocean and blew towards shore. Beaming, our father escorted her up the beach. She was like a real dove skimming across the sand, her soft sleek body landing near us on the porch as quietly, as gracefully, as a feather dropped from the sky.

"Happy Birthday," they both said, handing me their wrapped gifts.

It was obvious by now this was more than a birthday party. We all stood there, in the dream, none of us speaking, waiting for the groom to arrive. And when he did, bounding onto the porch with his large heavy strides, I realized to my horror that the man Dove was to marry was Joe Winter.

"I PREDICT you'll see him again," Robin assured Dove, his eyes wide and sincere. "I read it all in the cards last night."

He was speaking about Joe Winter. Mother had been pestering Dove all the previous week to stop by the restaurant, pick up her last paycheck, say her final good-byes. But Dove insisted she couldn't; it was all too sad. Perhaps she was fearful that once she was off the payroll, she would also be off his mind.

Now, already Monday again, our mother had given her an ultimatum. "You do it or I do it for you," she had said, and Dove had finally conceded.

"Don't worry," Robin said to her. "The cards don't lie."

"Do you really think so?" Dove asked. Of course she wasn't really asking Robin, wasn't waiting for a response.

We were eating breakfast around the table in the kitchen. Mother had risen early and made a batch of fluffy scrambled eggs and pancakes. I believe she actually felt some of Dove's sorrow, although she made it quite clear she was glad to be rid of Joe Winter.

"He's the worst kind of man," she had said. "Leading people on, making promises he never means to keep."

Still, she would not send Dove out on an empty stomach, or alone. She had told me to accompany my sister to the diner.

"That is what family is for," she reminded us as we ate. "To help one another through troubling times." But we had all had enough of those.

We dawdled over our meal. Dove particularly. She moved her eggs around her plate with the tines of her fork, let the butter atop her pancakes melt completely before pouring on maple syrup, then barely ate a bit.

"If you keep that up you won't get there before he opens up for business," mother said to Dove. "Now come on." She poured a large glass of milk, placed it on the table in front of Dove. "For the baby," mother said. "Drink up."

Dove heaved an enormous sigh, took another small bite of eggs, a sip of the milk.

"I wonder if the baby likes pancakes," I said.

"It's a boy," Robin said. "I forgot to tell you. I saw that in the cards too."

We ignored this last comment. Mother continued to hover around us while we ate, pushing my glass further from the edge of the table, wiping the top of the syrup bottle clean of drips. She corrected my grammar and reminded Robin to be home by nine, all the while watching Dove closely, as if she were really noticing her for the first time.

"Dove," she finally said. "Why don't you come to the movies tonight. There's a Robert Redford film playing. You haven't been to the theater in ages."

"He's too pretty for me," Dove said. "Besides I get cramps sitting for too long."

"Suit yourself," mother said. She banged two pans into the sink to be washed.

When Dove was finally ready to go, she scooted her chair back, rose from the table. "Come on Pigeon," she said to me. "Let's get this over with as painlessly as possible."

"Make sure he gives you all the money you're due," mother said from the sink. "Don't let him short you a day."

Then Dove and I were out the back door, letting the screen slam behind us, and we heard Robin call out "Good luck!" as we scrambled off the porch, our feet sinking into the still cool morning sand. Coming from someone like him, I figured that it really meant something

THE DINER was still dark when we arrived, the front door locked. It did not open for another two hours—on Mondays it was closed for breakfast—and Joe Winter set up for the lunch crowd by himself.

"We can get in around the back," Dove said.

I followed her around the side of the building, looked at the freshly painted wall for signs of the letters that had once proclaimed that Joe Loved Dove. Now, all that could be seen was the demarcation line where the old faded paint ended and the new fresh white-wash began.

The back door was unlocked and we walked into the whir-ring of the massive freezers, coolers, air conditioners, all working overtime in the heat. There was not the usual warm smell of food wafting from the stove and griddle—Dove told me that the cook did not get in until eleven on Mondays—but the antiseptic smell of scrubbed floors and stainless steel counters tops. Only one small light was on in the kitchen, and it took awhile for our eyes to adjust to the darkness after the brightness outside, for our ears to hear the sound of the radio playing a Bette Midler song over the din of the machinery. It was Dove's and Joe Winter's song—"Do You Want to Dance." Then we heard the sound of voices. It was two men talking low, whispering almost, and by the time we recognized who they were it was already too late.

There, pressed backward against the long counter top of the kitchen, naked from the waist up, was Uncle Edward. Standing in front of him, leaning towards him, face to face, chest to chest, was Joe Winter. He was fully dressed, but his right hand was out-stretched, his pointed finger extended. He weaved it among Uncle Edward's red chest hairs, then after licking his finger, traced the circle of each nipple with a damp thread of saliva.

They were talking to each other, or maybe merely singing the words to the song, familiar and close. But I could not get near enough to hear, before Dove had already pulled me away. Back past the freezers, out the door, and into the sun that felt all at once weighted and heavy on our shoulders and heads. She left her uni-form in a sad white heap outside the back door of the restaurant, along with her gold ankle chain.

Dove and I took an extremely circuitous route home. I followed her across the wide main street of town and then in the opposite direction of our house, towards the wealthy section where the houses were all newly built with white or cream-colored curved walls and large glass exteriors that opened up onto private pools, Jacuzzis, sheltered decks.

Although the sky was sunny and blue, no people lounged by these pools or decks in their swimsuits with their children, and there was no sign of life from the inside either, where I could see through the glass into plant-filled rooms and stainless steel kitchens. All was quiet, as if these houses were not really homes for people to live in, but only a strange part of the landscape that had been carved up out of the sand overnight by the ocean.

Trotting behind Dove, I found myself on a section of the beach I had never been before. It was here that she finally lay down on the sand for a moment, placed her hands across the part of her stomach where the baby lay, and breathed heavily, out of breath. Her face, in the sunlight, cast a shadow onto the sand, and I traced it with my finger, her small straight nose and chin, the long blonde eyelashes, the curve of her cheek.

"So he's gay too," she finally said. "I might have known. I should have known."

I looked at her, puzzled. I was not yet familiar with the term "gay."

"Joe loves Edward," Dove said, evoking the painted words on the side of the diner.

"He loves Uncle Edward?" I said.

Dove nodded.

"I thought he loved you."

She sat up and pointed towards one of the large white houses set back from the ocean. Its bleached deck curved around the house so that if sunbathing you could catch the rays from any angle. A four-car garage sat to one side, a tennis court on the other, and its massive glass windows shimmered at us and winked. There was even a second-floor balcony with high sheltered sides so that no one could see in.

"That's Joe Winter's house," Dove said.

"It is?" I said.

"There's a hot tub on that balcony where he took me one night. The water churned around us in a froth and we drank champagne right out of the bottle."

Dove took her hair in her hands and twisted it hard. With her foot, she smudged out the profile I had drawn of her in the sand.

"He showed me to a room all rose and sand colored," she continued. "With windows so large that the moon and the stars seemed to be beside me on the bed. He said that the house belonged to his family, but soon it would be his alone."

She blinked the wetness from her eyes. "He told me he only needed someone young to turn his life around, to change him. I didn't know he meant *a girl*," Dove said. "*Any girl*. I thought he meant *me*."

"You didn't love him, did you?" I asked her.

"Of course not," Dove said with a snort. "But don't you think that would have been a nice house for the baby to grow up in? Don't you think that would have been better than what we have?"

I didn't say anything, and Dove didn't seem to need an answer. I think she had already answered for herself.

Then we really did go home. Dove, directly to our room to be alone, and she did not come out all day, even for dinner. And she never did collect her last week's pay. Nor did we ever tell anyone about what we had seen. We barely even spoke about it between ourselves. It wasn't like it is today—people didn't speak openly of homosexuality back then. At least the people I knew. Certainly, at five, I had never heard of it, never even thought about it. Of course our mother knew, probably had always known about her brother, and Dove had known about Edward too. Maybe even Robin, who noticed things no one else did. But like so much in our lives, it had not been talked about or acknowledged in any way. Whether it was out of respect for Edward's privacy, a familial trait of secrecy, or just a blind eye to the truth, Edward's life had been kept hidden. Until that morning in the diner when we could not ignore what we had seen.

If I could not know my sister's feelings, it was because I barely knew my own. I did not want Uncle Edward to care for someone else, to look at someone else that way, the way I wanted him to look at me. But it was not that clear. I only knew I felt betrayed, and I felt that betrayal for my sister as well. At the diner, her anger and hurt had been palpable—on the surface of her skin—because she had been rejected for someone else. I don't believe this had ever happened to Dove before.

When I saw her that night, as I got myself ready for bed, she was not crying, although her eyes were red as if she had been, and she was sitting up at the desk where she had applied her makeup that morning. Only now she was scribbling away on a piece of paper with a ballpoint pen. Her head was bent studiously over her writing as if to shield it from my view, but as I approached, whispered good night, I could swear that it was a letter to Stan.

OVER THE next few days there was nothing to remind Dove and me of what we had seen at the diner. Uncle Edward did not come home, and Joe Winter's car was no longer pulling up out front to pick Dove up for work. Dove, who now had time on her hands, joined me on the beach, and we built elaborate sandcastles together. Surprisingly, even mother and Cary came out with us one Wednesday afternoon.

"I'm playing hooky," Cary told us. "It's too hot to work."

"Oh, you're so bad," mother said, giggling like a young girl.

She did not look like a young girl, though. In the bright unforgiving light of the beach, all the wrinkles under her eyes and around her lips were more pronounced. Her cheekbones were too sharp, there was a red vein on the side of her nose. I even spotted a gray hair at her temple.

If Cary noticed, he did not care. On a multi-colored beach blanket, he sat with his bare arm slung over her shoulders, buried her toes in the sand, even bent down and kissed her knees.

"Oh, Joanie," he murmured, and Dove and I looked away embarrassed.

For the most part, however, it was fun. Mother had made peanut butter and jelly sandwiches which we ate messily, crunching our teeth too often on sand, pretending it was only the peanuts. Cary had brought a Frisbee which he taught me to toss, all the while telling me it was a sport for sissies, girls. I discovered a jellyfish lying still damp and glistening, quivering in the sun, which all the other children on the beach came over to admire.

At one point in the afternoon, Cary boasted that he had gotten a tattoo in the army, and he offered to show it to us all.

"Oh, Cary," mother said. "You're terrible."

But he had piqued our interest. What did it look like? And since he wasn't wearing much, only his aqua bathing trunks, where was the tattoo?

"Show us," Dove said.

"Yes, show us," I echoed.

"Should I?" he teased.

Our mother covered her eyes with her hands. "Oh, really," she said.

Cary pulled his fingers through his short hair, flexed his arms like two wings.

"Come on," Dove prodded. "Quit stalling," and her face was all aglow.

"Oh, all right," Cary said. "Since you lovely ladies insist." Without waiting another moment, he turned his back to us, dropped his trunks a few inches, and there on the upper corner of his backside, was a small tattooed heart. Inside the heart, it read "Kiss my Ass."

"I simply don't know you," mother said, turning away.

"Well come on," he said to her. "Aren't you going to do it?"

But before we could move or say a word, he had pulled his suit back up, retied the drawstring at his waist, covered the tattoo once more.

By this time, Dove was on the sand rolling with laughter. She held her arms, curled her legs up like an infant. "Oh, it hurts," she said.

I do not believe she was really in pain. And, soon we were all doing it, falling onto the sand laughing, not really at the tattoo any-more, but for the pure happiness that we were all suddenly feeling. To be on the beach on a hot Wednesday afternoon in August, knowing that our summer days were numbered, yet for a while at least still able to enjoy the sun, the waves, and especially each other's company.

The Wedding

"Nothing good will ever come of this marriage," our mother warned Dove.

"But something is coming," Cary said, and he eyed Dove's growing stomach with an appraising smile.

"The marriage is doomed to failure," mother continued. "Two young strangers coming together for all the wrong reasons. Dove hasn't even finished high school!"

Nonetheless, Dove had already made up her mind. She and Stan would be married the first week in September, she told us. Right here in Uncle Edward's house by the municipal judge. She would wear a white dress, carry flowers, there would be a champagne toast. She, if no one else, had the wedding completely figured out.

It had, however, taken all the rest of us by surprise—Stan sauntering into the house one day just as unexpectedly as that evening way back in May when we were first introduced. Dove was waiting for him, sitting coolly on the bottom steps of the stairway, holding her knees with her arms so that you could not tell she was pregnant unless you already knew.

"I'm back," Stan said in his booming voice, entering our house without so much as a knock or a ring of the bell, and he swept Dove off the stairway and into his arms as if she were as light as the baby she carried inside.

It was a Thursday late afternoon and the rest of us—our mother, Robin, Cary, and I—were all sitting at the kitchen table eating the large cheese pizza that Cary had brought. The kitchen had become so familiar to me over the summer, it was as if we had always eaten there, at the six laminated chairs, the white curtain at the window, the small refrigerator and stove in the corner. Our mother's movie posters were still on the wall, my growing collection of seashells occupied their usual place on the back of the counter. There was a menu from Joe Winter's diner tacked up near the phone.

Today, the room was bright, Robin and Cary's chatter amusing, the pizza hot. I had already burnt the roof of my mouth on the cheese and was cooling it down with an ice cube I rolled between my teeth. Cary and Robin were having a race to see who could eat a slice the quickest, and melted cheese hung suspended in the air from their plates to their mouths, sauce dripping down their chins. Mother tried to reprimand us.

"Let's not eat like savages," she told us, but we ignored her; we had heard it before.

It was the distinctive sound of Stan's voice that made us finally stop what we were doing, look up, and we followed in amazement as he carried Dove into the kitchen, set her down on a chair, and then knelt before her on the linoleum floor.

"You've returned?" mother said.

"Forever," Stan said. From behind his back, he presented Dove with a single red rose and a diamond ring.

"Marry me," he said to her, as if we weren't all sitting there beside her, witnessing this event. Or as if it were intentional that we were—they might have been two actors in a dinner theater performing for their intimate audience. They ignored our comments, our eating, the sound of a damp glass filled with ice being placed on the table too quickly, too hard.

"Make me happy," Stan said.

"She's still in high school," mother said.

Cary reached across the table, into the flat box of pizza, pulled himself out another slice, shrugged his shoulders. "She's going to be a mother in a few months," he said.

At merely the mention of the word mother, Stan bent his large frame forward, kissed Dove on the stomach right where the baby was probably doing flips and handstands.

"If it's a girl we'll name the baby after you," he said to our mother. "Joan."

"Over my dead body," she said.

"Well, we're not going to name her after some stupid bird," Dove said.

"It might not even be a girl," Robin said, and I remembered that he had told us he had looked it up in the cards—the baby was to be a boy.

"That's true," Stan agreed. "This little lump could be a boy." Feeling brave, he lifted Dove's shirt for just a peek and kissed her stomach again on the bare flesh so that she giggled.

"I can't watch this," Robin said under his breath, but I could watch nothing else.

"Please be mine," Stan went on. "Don't turn me down again."

"I'd never be so dumb," Dove said. After placing the budded rose on the table, next to our pizza, she took from him the small blue velvet box he offered, snapped it open, and slipped the ring on her finger.

"That must have set you back a penny," Cary said.

"That's the most beautiful ring I ever saw," I said.

Dove held her finger up to the window, and let the diamond catch the sunlight coming through so that it formed a prism on the table and the wall. "I love it," she said.

"I guess that means yes," Stan said.

Dove, nuzzling her face in his arms, nodded in agreement.

They rocked together a moment, Stan kissing her hair, and when he looked up at us, a thin red wisp of it was still in his mouth, as if he were about to eat it.

"Dove's a hard nut to crack. I tried for weeks to convince her to marry me without any luck at all," he said.

"I suppose she had all her faculties intact at that point," mother said. She folded her arms across her chest, pinched her lips together tight. Unwittingly, Stan laughed as if she was making a joke, but of course we knew better.

She did not look at him, but at the display of movie publicity shots tacked up along the wall. She eyed the pizza cooling in its box, she gazed at the clock, and I even saw her dare a glance at Dove. It was a look of unbelieving pity.

"I know she's young," Stan said. "But she wrote me. She told me she was ready. And I'll make sure she finishes school. I'll make her go to college even." Kneeling there in front of the window, the sun hit the back of his light hair like a halo.

"Who would have guessed?" Cary said.

"I did," Robin said with wonder at his own foresight. "It was just as I predicted. She's getting married."

"Yes, married," Dove said, her voice clear and young, and full of promise. She was smiling and kissing the ring on her finger all at the same time. Her face had lost for a moment that pale wanness she had acquired during her pregnancy. "We're in love," she said.

"Love doesn't begin to cover what I feel for you," Stan said.

While Stan and Dove continued kissing, making their plans, mother skidded herself away from the table so that her chair made a screeching noise across the linoleum. Rising, she stacked all our dishes in her arms, although we were not through eating, and she walked over to the kitchen sink, let them all land there with a clatter.

"It's time to clean up," she ordered, but instead of running water from the tap, she stood there at the sink and rubbed her temples with her fingers as if she had a headache.

"Party pooper," Dove shouted after her, but Cary shook his head, hushed her with his finger, and, after examining our mother's tense curved back, he rose to join her, stood behind her, and placed his arms around her waist.

"Chill out, Joan," he said, as he pulled her towards him, but she pushed him away.

"She's such a fool," mother said.

She said it as if Dove and Stan were not right there in the room to hear; and it seemed to me then that we were often guilty of speaking that way in our family, as if our lives were all so segmented that what was said by one person could not possibly affect anyone else in the room. Like words held within cartoon balloons, only the characters were all from different comic strips, different pages.

"Joan," Cary was saying to her. "Calm down."

He caressed her cheek with his thumb. I was closest to the sink and I could hear Cary whisper to her that under the circumstances he was about as good as Dove could ever expect to do. The very best alternative.

"The man has a decent job, his own apartment," Cary said. "And he's a teacher, for Christ's sake."

"His first year," mother said.

"He's the father of her child," Cary said.

"But she's only seventeen." Her voice was strident and pained.

"That's about how old you were when you met Dad," Dove reminded her.

"A whole hell of a lot of good it did me," mother screamed back.

Rising from the floor at last, Stan placed one of his large hands on my head and the other on the top of Robin's head and gave us each an affectionate, if rather too vigorous, squeeze. "Let's not argue," he said. "Let's celebrate. Let's all go out together and celebrate."

"You've got to be kidding," mother said. Leaving the dirty dishes piled in the sink, she stormed out of the room.

To this day I barely know why our mother was so set against their marriage. Other than the fact that they were young, too young, it did seem the best possible solution for the coming baby. And it certainly seemed as if Stan was not only trying to do the right thing, but also truly loved Dove, would care for her and the baby always. Perhaps our mother knew something that I am unwilling to grasp even today—that love, although powerful and consuming, is never given in the right doses. It is either controlling and too binding, relinquished begrudgingly as if it were a painful sacrifice, or doled out in such a haphazard fashion that one is left bewildered, lost.

Or perhaps it was only that she saw for Dove a future too similar to her own, and wished for her daughter a different route and flight. I do know that it was the first time I ever really felt sorry for our mother. I wanted to promise her that things would be different, but I was silent as I watched her slender back as she walked away, her neck vulnerable below the short cropped red hair.

It was Cary who called after her. "Hey, we had a date," he said. "What about Brother Tank? He'll make you feel better."

At that, she turned around, spinning on one foot, almost slipping in her haste. "Don't you ever feel that life is just too goddamned sad?" she said.

Cary looked at her, puzzled.

"A meeting is not going to make me *feel better* tonight."

She did not attend Brother Tank's meeting that night, but instead went up to bed. And I noticed, after that, she saw Brother Tank far less frequently, spoke about him with much less fervor and zeal.

AFTER SHE was gone, Robin and I left Cary alone to do the dishes, Stan and Dove to continue their reconciliation elsewhere, and we went out to the back porch and sat on the steps facing the ocean.

It was early evening now and the sun was low in the sky, making the wet sand near the shoreline look almost like glass, smooth and reflecting the sky and the few scattered white clouds. There was a group of boys lying out in the ocean on their boogie boards waiting for waves; and when a good one came we watched them ride it in, their fingers gripped over the front of their boards, tight smiles slapped on their faces, their wet hair slicked back.

"I wish I had tried that this summer," Robin said. "It looks fun."

"It's not too late, is it?" I asked.

Robin shrugged regretfully.

Mothers had already begun gathering their children's sand toys from the beach, dropping them in mesh or canvas bags, shaking out towels and folding them, helping the youngest ones on with their flip-flops and sandals. The smooth low remains of sandcastles lay in various piles along the beach, and I heard one little girl announce loudly that no wave would ever destroy her castle. "It will stay here forever."

Although I was not much older than she was, I was able to laugh at her foolishness. "Hasn't she ever heard of tides?" I said to Robin, and rolled my eyes.

We sat there for a while in silence, as the summer moon rose too early, still competing for the sky with the sun, until Robin, unable to hold it in any longer (although we had each been thinking about it), at last spoke.

"You heard me, Pigeon, didn't you?" he said. "You heard me make that prediction that Dove would get married. I was right, wasn't I?"

"You have the gift," I said.

"I sure do," he agreed.

Then, although both of us were afraid to actually bring it up, we began wondering about the other prediction that Robin had made that day—the one about our father returning for the wedding—the one that meant anything at all. It seemed to me the much more difficult prediction of the two, the one more uncertain. Finally, I asked him.

"How will Daddy find out about the wedding?" I said. "How will he know when to come?"

Robin bit his lip, twitched somewhat in his light summer shirt that I noticed was stained with spots of pizza sauce. He considered an appropriate response. Before he could speak, though, we were interrupted by the sound of an ice cream vendor.

"Space Pops," he shouted. "Creamsicles, Fudgie Wudgie Bars."

He came, as if from out of the sand, out of the setting sun, carrying his large metal cooler in front of him, bumping it rhythmically against his thighs, and although it was late to be selling ice cream, he plodded up the beach toward our house.

"Creamsicles," he called. "Fudgie Wudgie Bars, ice cold Milky Ways. Space Pops."

When he finally reached us, we could see that he was a very old man, far older than the vendors we usually saw on the beach, and he was stooped from the weight of his cooler. He wore a white open-collared shirt and white hat with a black visor, and a grizzled two-day growth of beard. At the edge of our porch, he placed the metal cooler down on the sand. He looked at us straight on.

"Want any ice cream, kids?" he said.

When we peered at him through the sun, we could see he was missing his two top front teeth.

"Space Pops," he said. "Creamsicles, Fudgie Wudgie Bars, ice cold Milky Ways."

"We don't have any money right now," Robin explained in that patient way of his when he spoke to adults. Neither of us would have dared go into the house to ask for any.

"No, it's on me," the old man said, smiling, giving us another look at that black hole between his teeth. He flipped open the hinged metal top and reached down deep into the cooler so that his entire arm disappeared, as if it had been amputated, and pulled out two popsicles, a Creamsicle for me, a Fudge bar for Robin.

"They're my last two," he said, handing them to us.

I could feel the cold pop beneath the paper stinging pleasantly, and it stuck for a moment to my warm hand. When I pulled the wrapper back I could see a few small crystals clinging to its surface.

"Eat them in good health," he said. Then, almost as quickly as he had appeared, he was gone down the beach.

"Thank you," we shouted after him, and for an old man carrying a heavy load, he walked quickly, as if by ridding himself of those last two popsicles, his cooler had somehow, miraculously, become lighter. I wondered if he even heard us at all.

After he was gone, Robin and I concentrated on the business of eating our ice cream. We sucked on our pops, feeling their cold sweetness like a balm, not only on our throats, but inside us as well. We thought of the old man, of our good fortune, and when we finally looked at each other, we realized almost immediately and simultaneously, this had been the omen we were looking for. This was a sign.

"He's on his way here," Robin said, slurping rather too loudly. "Dad wrote that he'd be here for your birthday. Now he'll be making it for both events."

"Oh," I said, as I let the creamy orange flavor of the popsicle sit on my tongue until it melted away. "Of course he's coming." It was all beginning to sound a lot like my dream.

ALTHOUGH IT was already September, the day Dove and Stan had chosen to get married was one of the hottest days I could remember all summer. By late morning, we were all in various states of distress. Uncle Edward, who had ordered flowers and a huge cake, and arranged for caterers to come with food tables, pink cloths, and napkins, worried that everything would either wilt, melt, or spoil in the hot sun.

"We'll be drinking warm champagne, staring at dead flowers, and we'll all come down with ptomaine poisoning," he predicted.

"No, no, no," said one of the caterers. "Don't worry about a thing. This is our profession."

Nonetheless, Uncle Edward carted a large fan from inside out on the back porch, and plugged it in with an extra long extension cord in an effort to cool everything down. As if he believed he could fan the entire outdoors.

"No, no, no," said the caterer again. "It isn't necessary."

"It works for me," said Uncle Edward.

Our mother, in the kitchen, sat at the table dressed only in a robe, pressing an ice-cold compress against her forehead.

"I don't know why I let them talk me into having it here," she groaned.

Of course, no one had talked our mother into anything. It had been entirely Dove's idea, and it was Uncle Edward, calling it a splendid suggestion, who had agreed on the spot to foot the entire bill. He told Dove to select the bridal gown of her dreams and he promised me a new dress as well.

"Can't have you wearing Robin's old jeans or gym shorts to the wedding, can we?" he had said.

"I guess not," I agreed.

Considering what we had seen that one morning at the diner, Dove appeared to have little remorse about accepting all the money from Uncle Edward.

"He owes it to me," she said. "Don't you think?"

I was not convinced. It might have been easier for me to understand if we had actually confronted him with what we had seen—the two of them together like that. But, we had never told anyone about it, making it easier and easier to believe it had never taken place. Being young, I even wondered if what I thought I saw was what it really was, if that had even been Uncle Edward in the kitchen shirtless, if we had watched them in that strange embrace. Or if it had all been made up, a product of Dove's imagination, a ruse needed for her to justify finally marrying Stan.

"Of course, they're having an affair," she said to me when I expressed my doubts. "They're both just too chicken shit to admit it."

Not even ten years later, of course, it became the vogue for men to discuss their sexual persuasions out loud, but Uncle Edward would never become that kind of man. As long as I knew him, and I knew him the rest of his life, he never once let on—he was always going away on business, visiting an acquaintance in New York, helping his good friend Joe Winter with some financial matters—and would only sometimes sit sadly telling us he was thinking of the children, of the family, he never had.

The morning of the wedding, Dove lay in the bathtub flat on her back with her knees sticking straight up in the air. She allowed only me in the room, and then only on the condition that I constantly replenish her glass of iced tea.

"Look at me," she said as I sat on the toilet seat. "I'm a beached whale." She stared at her stomach, which protruded just a bit above the water line.

"You do look pregnant," I said.

"Pregnant," she repeated. "I look like I'm giving birth to quintuplets, to an elephant child. Stan will probably back out when he gets a look at me in my dress," she said.

But that was impossible to believe.

Stan had been at our door at nine in the morning, already completely dressed in a beautifully tailored dark blue suit and a flowered silk tie, although the ceremony was not called until noon. He wore a white rosebud in his lapel, and carried a huge bouquet of summer blooms, although our house would soon be brimming with the flowers Uncle Edward had already ordered.

Bouncing from toe to heel, heel to toe, he shouted throughout the house, "Where's my bride? Where's my beautiful bride?"

Even after mother silenced him with a cup of coffee and the admonishing words that Dove was still asleep, he could not be discouraged. He asked me to check on her each half-hour, straightened his tie a half dozen times, combed his hair. Now, at a quarter to eleven, he was still waiting at the house for his bride to show. He stood on the porch, leaning against one of the posts, humming the wedding march under his breath, and in the midst of the caterer's activity, of Uncle Edward's hysteria, and our mother's cold compress, her inertia, Stan alone remained as cool and as happy as if he had just stepped out from a dip in the ocean.

I wish I could have remained so calm. It was hot enough outside, but inside, with the caterers using the oven, it was worse, and the strong odor of the flowers was too overpowering for the small house. In addition, mother had me running from one end to the other.

"Get me my shoes," she ordered. "Go make sure all the front windows are open," and over and over, "Get your sister out of the tub."

Most of all, though, it was the dress. Uncle Edward had bought it for me; it was a pale peach dress, sleeveless, with a scooped neck. It scratched under my arms, smelled too new, and although I had tried it on many times since we had brought it home, I was each time newly convinced that it made me look too tall and gawky, my arms and legs like thin sticks. I could not have our father seeing me after all these months looking like this.

"Like a young colt," Uncle Edward had insisted. "Like a free-spirited young colt."

"Like a horse," Robin chimed in.

And that was how I saw myself the morning of the wedding, like a horse with skinny legs and a long face. I would never be beautiful like Dove, nor psychic like Robin—I would only be the youngest.

By eleven-thirty, the guests began to arrive, and I examined each of them, knowing their approach only meant our father's arrival was that much sooner. Joe Winter was first, carrying an enormous box wrapped in white paper and a bow.

"For the lovely bride and the lucky groom," he said, setting it down on the table in the living room. "May they have one hell of a wedding night."

Some of the waitresses who had worked with Dove were next, and after their girlish chatter of garters and trousseaus came some people I did not recognize, who I later learned were colleagues of Stan's at the university. There were four of them, three men and one woman, and they moved together as if in some unusual and awkward dance, and said hello, and congratulations, almost in unison. Later, throughout the ceremony, I heard them discussing our small beach community—the overdevelopment of the Jersey shore, the erosion of dunes, syringes washing up onto the sand.

Cary arrived too, of course, wearing the seersucker suit I had first seen him in, carrying his tie and jacket over his shoulder.

"It's a scorcher out there," he said to me. "Hotter than Hades, isn't it?" and, slipping his hand into his back pocket, he pulled out a small Chinese fan decorated with butterflies and lilies.

"For you, my little Pigeon," he said. "So that you'll always be cool."

There were other guests as well, whom I was not introduced to, did not know—the man our mother worked for at the movie theater and his wife, three followers of Brother Tank, a few friends of Stan's from his college days.

Arriving at the house last of all were Stan's parents and his younger sister Amelia, and I was surprised to find that they were not giants, but normal-sized people, with average handshakes, mere mortal smiles. His parents looked as if they had once been rather handsome, but now their faces were faded and grey. His father wore outdated glasses, and his suit was just a bit too tight, as if he had only lately gained weight.

Stan's mother's hair was curled stiff with hair spray and there were damp spots already at the arms of her dress. It was Amelia, though, who attracted the most attention. She was not particularly pretty, too busty, her nose too long, lips too wide. But her face was heavily made up and she wore a short tight black summer shift that prompted a second look from Joe Winter.

"Look at those legs," I heard him say under his breath. "Look at that ass."

Uncle Edward, not our mother, took Stan's family under his wing, introduced them all around, and then eased them out onto the back porch with pleasantries and congratulations; and for a while, until the ceremony began, they stood there moving only occasionally in the same spot, looking over-heated and uncomfortable.

Surprisingly, it was Robin who finally came to the rescue.

"I'd like to read your palms," he said in his quiet polite voice. "That is, if you don't mind."

I believe they were at first quite taken aback, but then out of curiosity, they submitted to Robin's reading. They sat down at one of the pink tables in the shade of the porch, and huddled close like four people arranging a business deal.

I did not hear what Robin said in its entirety, but instead bits and pieces of what he foresaw for these three strangers who were soon to be related to us in that most bizarre of kinships—in-laws. It was the first time I had ever seen his psychic powers in motion.

"Your left hand is the hand of promise," I heard Robin say to Stan's mother. "And look at your Mount of Venus—you will surely cry at this wedding."

To Stan's father, he warned him about poor digestion. "You must learn to eat more healthily," Robin advised. "And your worry lines are deep and numerous."

"I have a lot to worry about," Stan's father said, and Stan, listening too from the edge of the porch, shook his head laughing.

"Me next," Amelia said, anxious to have her palm read too. "Who will I marry?" she asked Robin; then, with a glint in her eye, "How many men?"

Robin giggled self-consciously. "I can't predict that," he said. But holding her palm up close to his face, he studied it, and smiled. "You have a lot of enthusiasm," he said to her. "That's evident in Jupiter. But you're a bit out of control."

"I could have told you that," said Stan's father. "They're all out of control."

"Shhh," said his wife. "Do stop that."

Robin put them both at ease. "Now don't worry," he said. "I see Amelia marrying late in life. Opting for freedom early on."

"Great," said Stan's father. "Just great."

And Stan, moving towards them all in an encompassing embrace, slapped his father on the back. "Isn't it wonderful having a psychic in the family," he said. "It's just what we always needed."

When the municipal judge arrived, all the gathered guests grew silent and assembled out on the porch where Uncle Edward had placed a particularly large display of flowers.

They sat on the folding chairs that had been set up, wiping their hot brows, fanning the still air with clutched pieces of paper, Mozart filtering out from a tape being played inside. Stan hurried off to join his bride. I began for the first time that morning to really panic.

"Where's Daddy?" I hissed at Robin who had taken a front row seat. "Why isn't he here yet?"

I had certainly not expected him to arrive early, nor even at the same time as the other guests, but to make his entrance solo and grand. But it was getting too late even for that.

The soft harpsichord music was playing. Stan's parents were standing next to him in front of the judge. Mother stood on the opposite side in a yellow dress looking as if she might faint from the heat; her lips trembled, her body wavered, but she managed to hold her ground.

"Daddy's going to miss the ceremony," I hissed. "He won't see them get married."

"What do you want me to do," Robin whispered back, but I could tell he too was upset.

Then Dove, escorted by Uncle Edward, walked out of the house and onto the porch, and I could no longer worry about our father, but could only watch my sister get married.

Her long red hair was down, and wreathed with flowers; you noticed that first. Her beautiful face was poised, calm. She floated, not walked, in her white flat slippers, and wore a floor-length cotton dress with a simple neckline, large puffed sleeves, and a lace train that fell gracefully in the back. You could, of course, tell she was pregnant by the slight rise in the front of the dress, but it seemed a more natural state than it ever had in the past, as if all brides should be glowing and pregnant, proving that their love had already made a lasting impression, that it was not something fleeting that could ever be forgotten or left behind.

Uncle Edward, beside her, played the perfect father. In fact, there may have been some who actually thought he was; with his red hair and coloring, his handsome face, he looked so similar to Dove. But he wasn't our father. Our father had not arrived. And I was certain, watching my sister walk forward to get married, that I would never see him hereafter. None of us would. Nor would I ever again experience or believe in the safety I had once enjoyed as a little pigeon being sung softly to sleep.

When Dove finally reached Stan, the music stopped and she took her place beside him. Our mother, standing to her left, pressed her hand in Uncle Edward's. Their eyes were damp as they too obviously stared away from the ceremony and towards the ocean where the waves crashed into white foam, then slipped away.

The judge, white-haired and dressed in a black robe, began to speak of commitment and trust, the security two people can provide for each other, the unbreakable marriage bond. I listened as closely as if he were speaking to me, without coughing or fidgeting, and managed not to cry out that it was all a lie. Marriages break up, I wanted to shout. Fathers can abandon their children, children can be left alone. There is nothing in the vow that is sacred. There is no security—we are each of us alone.

Later on, as an adult, I would recognize that moment at Dove and Stan's wedding as an awakening—when I realized for the first time that no matter what the judge said, no matter how much we all might like it differently, our parents, our loved ones, are not ours forever, and we are not theirs to keep. There is always a chink in the armor, an unraveling of the ties, we are always at last on our own. As a result, I find it difficult to believe in marriage, to make that commitment towards a future that I know so little about, to trust in a person I can know only remotely, to trust that person will care for me, look after me. It is not that I don't believe in love—I do, I do. But I know that if you were to ask me, I would tell you—I am just looking after Pigeon.

Stan placed the ring on Dove's finger, and she placed one on his. Stan's mother heaved an enormous sigh, his father smiled. Our mother and Uncle Edward wore the tight expressions they had worn all morning. In the background the waves roared and heaved as they moved toward low tide, and two seagulls swooped down to pick up some scrap from the sand. A girl tossed a Frisbee to her friend, a mother called to her young son, and an ice cream vendor passed by, not the old one we had seen the other day, but a teenaged boy. The judge cleared his throat and pronounced Stan and Dove husband and wife. They paused a moment to listen to the sounds from the beach, and then they kissed.

"You wouldn't believe she's about to have a baby," I heard one of the waitresses whisper behind me. She had twisted her long hair and pulled it up so that her neck might catch a breeze, if there were a breeze. "Dove looks so lovely."

"And what a catch he is," her neighbor whispered back. "I heard he has a cute little apartment in the city."

They watched as Dove and Stan clutched each other in an embrace that went on too long, particularly in that hot afternoon sun; they both sighed. And I heard little else the rest of the day.

I am sure we all enjoyed the food, the champagne toast, the dancing in the hot sand; I remember none of it. I only recall what happened much later in the day, after the party was well underway. It began to rain. Not just a light summer rain, but a heavy downpour, as if the sky had finally been slit open by the tremendous heat of the day and a torrent of water had spewed forth. Lightning flashed wickedly and thunder rumbled close to my ears.

People on the beach scrambled for cover. And we at the reception hurried under the roof of the porch, carrying in our hands our plates of food, a bottle of wine, a blossoming centerpiece.

The party ended quickly after that. Women screeched about their hair, as their light summer dresses became nearly transparent. Uncle Edward scurried around with the caterers, carrying platters of food stacked high into the house, closing down the bar, folding up chairs. The pink cloths, when lifted from the tables, flapped like wet flags in the wind.

"I knew something like this would happen," Stan's father moaned as he and his family dashed away towards their car.

"Stop that complaining," his wife said. "Didn't you hear what that boy told you? That fortune-teller."

And Amelia, who carried a glass of wine in each hand, kicked off her shoes and giggled almost hysterically at her parents' discomfort.

Huddled around a tray of crudités, forgotten and still left out, stood the people from the university, reluctant even in the rain to head back to the city, to leave behind all the food.

"Stop talking about pesticides," I heard the woman remark to her colleagues. "I haven't eaten food like this in weeks."

And Joe Winter, in his usual manner, herded a number of young women into his car, and although the convertible's top was still down, they rode off that way down the street in the pouring rain.

I looked for Robin, but he had already gone up to his room earlier, right after the ceremony. Edward was inside with the caterers, and, at the rapid disappearance of all the guests, our mother followed suit, leaving her wet uncomfortable high-heeled shoes at the bottom of the stairs.

"I'm going to bed," she called down to me, although it was still afternoon.

Her mascara had made dark circles around her eyes, and her head looked small and sleek like a seal's.

I thought she was going to say more, something about the wedding or the rain, but she only looked at me wearily before disappearing into her room, and I did not see her again until the next morning.

Outside, at the edge of the porch, Stan and Dove stood together looking out towards the sea and the rain.

"What a send-off," Stan said. "A thunderstorm."

"Isn't it romantic," said Dove.

He scooped Dove up, lifted her into his arms, and carried her like that as he walked off the porch and down onto the beach. Stan's shoes made a squelching sound, as Dove's lace train, heavy with water, caught on something in the sand and was left behind.

They did turn once and wave to me, and Dove tossed her bouquet, although it landed far from where I stood; and then they kept walking, as if it weren't raining at all, or even more likely, as if this had all been planned by them, as part of the entertainment, as essential a finale to a wedding as thrown rice, a decorated car.

Soon, it was only Cary and me still remaining outside. Cary's blue-and-white seersucker jacket hung limply and wet. His hair was plastered so close to his scalp he looked almost bald.

"Well, Pigeon," he said to me, mopping his round wet face with his handkerchief. "They say rain is good luck on a wedding day. But I think that's all a crock. What about you?"

"I don't know," I said.

"I think it was made up to make the bride feel better," Cary went on. "When she knows deep down inside that the rain sucks and it's ruined everyone's hair and clothes. Good luck—like who are they kidding?"

I shrugged my shoulders.

Looking down at my own peach dress, I saw that it too had been damaged from the storm. Its hem dragged a bit, the sleeves curled up, but it did not make me unhappy. Instead, I only wanted to be rid of it, and although I had not done anything so immodest and childlike in years, I pulled off my shoes, tugged the wet dress up over my head, and tossed it onto the ground, leaving me standing there dressed only in my new white slip.

Cary blinked his eyes. "You stripping out here?" he said.

"It feels good," I said. And it did; the slip was light after the constricting dress, and I felt suddenly cool and free.

"I'll just bet it does," Cary said, and, laughing, he kicked off his shoes, slipped out of his own jacket, and, unbuttoning his shirt, he took that off too. "You're right," he said. "It does feel good."

Only half-dressed, we walked out to where the rain slid off the roof of the porch in a large sheet, and let it fall down around us like a waterfall.

Through the rush of the water, we could hear Uncle Edward calling out to us from the back door. "What are you two doing? Get dressed. Come inside." And when we did not immediately respond, "Are you crazy?"

But neither of us had any intention of obeying his orders. We simply stood out there, happy to be no longer dressed for a wedding, and let the rainstorm take its natural, if unlucky, course.

IT WAS uncanny, but two days after Dove and Stan's wedding I actually heard from our father. It was a package sent from a New York City postmark and this time it was addressed solely to me. I carried the box into the kitchen where our mother tore through the packing tape with a knife, and when we pulled the top flaps open, white Styrofoam popcorn tumbled out. Mother reached in with two hands, deep below the protective Styrofoam, and pulled out for me another box, this one wrapped in shiny pink paper and tied with a large white bow.

It was an early birthday present, it turned out, with a card that read: "For my darling Pigeon, Happy 6th Birthday. Love, Daddy." There was no mention of him coming to visit soon, or at all, or of a birthday celebration with cake and ice cream. There was nothing in it to reveal that he had ever promised to return, that he had sent postcards telling us he was on his way, would be there soon, missed us terribly.

"Aren't you going to see what he sent?" mother asked. She was looking at me anxiously, but kindly. She picked up the package, held it in front of her eyes, turned it twice around. "Looks promising," she said.

I nodded, and although I had always loved receiving presents in the past, I opened this one methodically, and without enthusiasm, carefully taking off first the ribbon, then scraping away at the scotch tape, so that the wrapping paper would not tear. Inside, on top, there lay an ornately packaged box of Belgian chocolates, the kind with creamy centers that sat lightly on your tongue and slowly and deliciously melted.

"Just like your father," mother said.

But it was beneath the candy that the real gift lay. It was a white cotton eyelet dress, with pink trim ribboned through the sleeves, collar and hem. It had a dropped waistband and a pale pink rose embroidered just below the neckline.

It was the most beautiful dress I had ever seen, and mother and I both audibly sighed at the sight. Our pleasure, however, was short lived, for it was apparent as soon as I held the dress up before me that it was far far too small, and that even with alterations would never fit, never even go over my head. It was a dress meant for a much younger and petite girl, certainly not for one with my long arms and legs, broad shoulders.

"It does seem rather small," mother said, taking a sleeve of the dress, tugging on it as if that would make it magically larger.

"It's for a baby," I said. "He bought it for a baby," and then I burst into tears, crying all over the white dress that would never be worn, but that would sit in its box for almost twenty years. It traveled with me to college and to my first apartment; and even recently, when the man I live with found it yellowed and faded on top of my closet and laughed at my utter foolishness, I still did not have the heart to throw it away.

That afternoon, though, I would have given anything to wear that dress, to have had it fit, and knowing it never would only made me cry harder. Our mother looked at me hopelessly for a few minutes, with a puzzled, wide-eyed look on her face, and then, seeing that I was only growing more hysterical, she finally took me in her arms.

It was an awkward gesture with none of the simple ease that some mothers have with their daughters, but it came to me like a warm wool blanket on a cold night. I curved into her, felt my body shake with sobs, and held onto her arm with all my strength and might.

Later that night she wrapped the dress back up in the tissue paper, and I put it away on the top of the first of many closets. I even grew so generous as to share the chocolates with everyone in the house. Uncle Edward told me that the only time he had ever had chocolates so good was in Europe; Robin ate five, Cary three, and even our mother conceded and ate one.

"See what your sister is missing," mother said. "She could have had these chocolates from your father too."

"I think she got what she wanted," Cary said.

"Stan," Robin added. "She got Stan."

Due to Dove's pregnancy, they had not gone on a honeymoon after the wedding, but had driven later in the day back to Stan's apartment in the city. We had never seen where Dove was to live, but she assured us it was a cozy place with a study that could easily be transformed into a nursery. She told us there was a park nearby where she and the baby could play while Stan was busy teaching; and at the end of the day she would wheel the baby over to Stan's office in one of the university buildings and they would walk home together. Later, she could leave the baby at the daycare center that the university provided, and she would go back to school to finish her last year.

"So that's what you think it's going to be like," mother had said.

"I know it," Dove answered.

"That's a fairy tale," mother warned.

"You're right about that," Dove had said, and the next afternoon she had called us on the phone just to remind us how really happy she was.

Now eating the chocolates, with Dove so obviously missing, we could not help but think about her. I thought of how my family was shrinking, first our father gone, now Dove. Perhaps our mother or Uncle Edward next. It was not easy to determine how much longer Cary would stick around.

Soon we would all be off in different places—this summer at the beach was only the beginning—and our lives would touch through long-distance phone calls, the rare visit, and of course, the occasional picture postcard with a short message, the foreign post date. It did not make me sad, however, as it had in the past—it only made me wonder what flight was in store for me.

Uncle Edward put his arm around me on the couch, stroked my hair. "She and Stan are going to start their own life now," he said.

"And soon the baby too," Cary chided. "Let's not forget the baby."

"I pray to God it works out for them," Uncle Edward said.

"Your prayers don't have a chance," said mother.

But I joined Uncle Edward anyway, and said one silently, for all of us.

That was really the end of the summer. One week later, I started first grade in the local public school. Taking the bus with Robin, I sat next to him on the seat and knew once again my life was about to change through no fault of my own, without even foresight from Robin on how it would all turn out.

After the wedding, he had stopped working for Edith, stopped seeing her altogether. I suppose it was because his prediction about our father had been wrong, but he never said this.

"Who am I fooling," he had said, instead. "It was all guesswork, anyway." He had gone back to wanting to be a doctor, a surgeon no less. "Doctors not only predict, they *make* the future. That's what I'm going to do." And that was another prediction my brother made that would ultimately come true.

Now sitting beside me on the bus, he bit his lip, worried that he did not know a single other child, and yet reassured me nonetheless.

"You're going to love school, Pigeon," he said.

"I don't know," I said.

The bus screeched around corners, driven by a scowling woman with a severe haircut—she looked as if she could eat children for breakfast—and there was a broken spring in the seat right under my left leg that was already giving me a cramp.

"You're smart," Robin went on. "You already know how to read. You know lots of things the other kids don't. You'll do well. And you'll make lots of friends."

I looked at the other children on the bus; some appeared to be my age, and they, like me, sat beside older brothers and sisters, clutching their lunch boxes, staring longingly out the window as their mothers, their houses, and then the beach, dissolved from view.

One girl in front of us, with two curly pigtails, even pinched her nostrils between two fingers, peered between the seats back at me.

"It stinks in here," she said. "This bus smells like sour milk."

Agreeing, I pinched my own nostrils shut. "It sure does," I said, feeling a kinship unlike anything I had felt before.

"You gotta hold your nose really tight," she advised.

"I am," I said smiling.

I realized suddenly school would be new not only for me, but for many of us. Our first opportunity to compare ourselves to someone outside our own family, to finally see the shortcomings, the idiosyncrasies, the difference. Together, we children would all travel there on this old hurtling bus, frightened and unknowing, and yes, also eager to show each other just how well we could certainly survive.

Afterword

I suppose I should add that eight years later, we received word of our father's death.

I was the only child home at that time. Robin was away at college, Dove was still married to Stan, with a son of their own, and after my mother gave the short letter to me, I read it over a few times to myself before putting it back in its envelope.

It was addressed to our mother, although it might have been to anyone, any mere acquaintance, for all the specific details it contained. It said only that our father had suffered from lung cancer in a hospital in Chicago for two months until finally succumbing to the illness. He had not died alone; the letter was from a woman he had been living with.

She had sat by his hospital bed with him, watching him deteriorate as the cancer spread through his body. The way a wife would, she wrote, and added at the end that she regretted the fact that he had never divorced our mother.

I am ashamed to say that I did not cry at the news. Nor do I remember thinking about it for long. I simply went about the rest of my day as if nothing unusual had occurred. It was a Friday and I went to school, and even spent the weekend at a friend's house; and when I told her of my father's death she was shocked at my nonchalance, my indifference.

Not the man who sits next to me tonight. He has read much of this over my shoulder as I wrote it down, quickly, and without stopping for food or thought, or barely air.

"I'm surprised you don't hate him," he tells me.

"Hate him?" I ask, puzzled. The word seems far too strong for anything I might still feel for my father.

"For what he did to you," he says to me. "He abandoned you. Don't you despise him for that?"

I don't, but it is certainly not through lack of trying—I tell him that—this man who strokes the side of my face and asks me these difficult questions in our darkening room.

He is a man who likes to solve riddles and acrostic puzzles, he believes in God, and right and wrong, feels there is only one answer to each question. He approaches problems like a surgeon with a scalpel, cutting away at the damaged flesh. He believes he can still help me.

And I hope that he can. Perhaps I lied back there when I wrote of Dove and Stan's wedding, of taking care of myself. In some strange way I will always be searching for our father, the childhood I longed for. I believe it is what we all try to do—somehow replace what we felt we missed while we were young. As if it could be replaced, as if there is someone who could look after us. Still, we want it just the same.

I kiss my man in the places I know he loves best, and try to explain this to him.

"Rest assured," I tell him as my lips feel the warmth of his neck. "It does not diminish anything I feel for you."

"I know that," he says.

Later that night, as we fall asleep, our legs are joined, his fingers curl loosely in my hair. I feel the weight of his body on the bed beside me. We are connected and close.

"This is surely enough. More than enough," I whisper to his closed eyes and believe it. Still I pray, with the fervor of a true convert, that what I say be true.